CONSTANCE

BY THE SAME AUTHOR

Blood and Water and Other Tales
The Grotesque
Spider
Dr Haggard's Disease
Asylum
Martha Peake: A Novel of the Revolution
Port Mungo
Ghost Town: Tales of Manhattan Then and Now
Trauma

CONSTANCE

PATRICK MCGRATH

BLOOMSBURY CIRCUS

LONDON · NEW DELHI · NEW YORK · SYDNEY

First published in Great Britain 2013

Copyright © 2013 by Patrick McGrath

The moral right of the author has been asserted

Bloomsbury Circus is an imprint of Bloomsbury Publishing Plc
50 Bedford Square
London
WC1B 3DP

www.bloomsbury.com

Bloomsbury Publishing, London, New Delhi, New York and Sydney
A CIP catalogue record for this book is available from the British Library

ISBN 978 1 4088 2113 8

10 9 8 7 6 5 4 3 2 1

Typeset by Hewer Text UK Ltd, Edinburgh
Printed and bound in Great Britain by CPI Group (UK) Ltd, Croydon CR0 4YY

For my sister, Judy; and, as ever, for Maria

ONE

MY NAME IS Constance Schuyler Klein. The story of my life begins the day I married an Englishman called Sidney Klein and said good-bye forever to Ravenswood and Daddy and all that went before. I have a husband now, I thought, a new daddy. I intended to become my own woman. I intended, oh, I intended everything. I saw myself reborn. Gone forever the voice of scorn and disapproval, the needling, querulous voice so unshakable in its conviction that I was worthless, worse than worthless, *unnecessary*. Sidney didn't think I was unnecessary and this was a man who knew the world and could recite Shakespeare by heart. He said he loved me and when I asked him why, he said, Better ask why the sky is blue. It changed everything. If before I trod the streets of New York City with the diffident step of a stranger, I exulted now in all that had so recently troubled me, the crowds, the speed, the noise, the voices.

Others recognized the change in me. The editor in chief guessed my secret at once. She told me I was in love. I tried to deny it for it hadn't occurred to me that that was what was happening but she insisted. She said she should know what it looked like and I asked her what that was. Like you, she said, and walked away with an inscrutable smile on her lips. Another time she asked me if I was finding fulfillment in my work and I told her that I was. You hold on to it then, she said. I assumed she meant I couldn't love Sidney Klein and my job at the same time but I told her I could. Ellen Taussig was able to speak a volume with the small motion of an eyebrow. But it's true, I cried softly. Why shouldn't I? Many are called, she said, and peered over her spectacles at me. It's a telling indication of what I felt then, that my confidence was unshaken even by the wealth of skepticism in that arch plucked eyebrow.

Then came the wedding.

It was only afterward, after the lunch in a restaurant, with my sister Iris disgracing herself, and Daddy being so angry, that I asked myself just what I thought I was doing. Who did I think I was, a proper person? The new world crumpled like a balled sheet of paper thrown in the fire and I was left with a few charred remnants and some ash. In my diminishment and humiliation I thought of Sidney's mother, a little twisted rheumatic madwoman who'd shown up for our wedding dressed all in black. I was a shriveled thing like her. I was Sidney's mother. I tried to tell him what had happened but he didn't want to hear it. It didn't conform to his idea of me. It was the first time I saw this clearly, and seeing it, I realized how foolish I'd been to think I might for even an instant have believed I'd be *loved*—

Sidney's apartment was large and dark and full of books. I didn't like it. I found it intimidating. Everything in it seemed to tell me that here lived a clever person, a *proper* person. I felt that at any moment I'd be unmasked as a trespasser and evicted. It was on a high floor of a prewar building on the Upper West Side and it was always very noisy at night. Everything was changing, Sidney told me, as the old residents began to move out to the suburbs and the poor moved in, the blacks and the Puerto Ricans, the immigrants, the newcomers. There were rough, raw, foreign voices in the street and I had the unsettling sensation of living in two worlds at once, neither of which I belonged to or was a part of.

Sidney had acquired the apartment during his first marriage, which had ended in divorce. There was a child from that marriage, a boy called Howard who lived with his mother in Atlantic City. Sidney often went to see them and was clearly fond of the boy but I felt no desire to know him. I preferred that Sidney not talk about him. Howard already had a mother. Meanwhile I was becoming increasingly troubled as to why he'd chosen me for a wife. When I asked him he made a joke of it. He said I'd looked so bewildered at that book party on Sutton Place he thought he should rescue me before I screamed.

Then for a time I was happy, or as happy as I was capable of being in the circumstances. Sidney stood at the margins of my day. He was the man with whom I awoke in the morning and to whom I returned after work in the evening, and with whom I went to bed at night. But I was no longer at peace in my mind and I grew uneasy with the terms of the marriage as established by him. I don't understand how it happened and I tried not to be obsessive about it but I began to think I'd made a mistake, and that none of it was meant for me, it was meant for someone else. One of the difficulties I'd foreseen when he first proposed to me was that he knew so much more than me and after a while this grew irksome. Poor Sidney, he loved to teach me. He wanted to give me all the knowledge he possessed and he was annoyed when his generosity wasn't appreciated. I told him I'd been educated already.

—Ha! he shouted. He sat forward. His eyes were hot with disdain. Oh, you have, have you? he said.

This was vicious and it hurt me. It was just the sort of thing Daddy would say. Sidney preferred students who after a certain amount of argumentation backed down but this time I didn't back down, I'd had enough of being spoken to like that. It was our first real quarrel and I frightened myself with the things I said. I told him he was an old man and he was too fat and he'd been cruel to make me marry him. Later I clung to him in bed, appalled at what I'd said. He comforted me. He told me that my urge to defy him was really an expression of love. I seized on this idea but later I realized I didn't believe it. I didn't say this to him but it confirmed my suspicion that he had no real interest in who I was, only in how I conformed to the image of me he'd constructed in his mind. At times I felt like a ghost in that apartment.

Another time he asked me if I would read some galley proofs for him.

—You think I don't have work of my own? I said.

—I'll pay you.

I'll pay you. I was beginning to understand why I'd agreed to marry him. Daddy never gave me what I needed and I felt it was my fault. Children take responsibility for whatever befalls them, good or ill. In my case, ill. From the moment I'd met Sidney I'd wanted *him* for a daddy so I could start over. But you can't do it! It's an absurd idea on its face! What a fool I'd been to believe it might be different. But by the time I realized this it was too late, I was already Mrs. Klein. Or Mrs. Schuyler Klein.

Another problem was his assumption that I shared his impatience to start a family. I don't know why I was so resistant to the idea. Most women want to have children, why not me? Perhaps it was connected to his sexual demands. I wasn't *violently* opposed to the idea, I mean of having a child, but I think now it was another expression of the power struggle that was becoming a constant dissonant whisper in the background of the marriage. Sidney wrote, and he lectured, and he was often away at conferences: He was a busy man and much in demand. What would happen if there was a child in the apartment? I knew what would happen, I'd have to give up my job, and I wasn't prepared to do that. I remember asking him if his father had been conscientious in the home. He told me that no, his father left the work of the household to the women. So why was he different?

—I thought it through, he said.

He thought everything through. At times he exhausted me with his thinking. He had a precise, logical mind that functioned with impressive quickness but he wasn't *creative*. He could never have written a poem, for example. He could subject a poem to critical analysis but that's as far as it went. He lacked imagination.

In those days he liked to bring his students home and there were frequent loud frightening arguments in the sitting room.

Because it was a big apartment, and because we were careless in this regard, a condition of chronic untidiness prevailed. Only the efforts of Gladys arrested our descent into a state of true squalor, Gladys being Sidney's housekeeper, a good Christian woman from Atlanta, Georgia, as he liked to say. And although I was always too tired to join in these discussions he organized in his home I never objected. I just went to the bedroom but I was unnerved by the sound of muted talk and raucous laughter, although I didn't complain about it. But I couldn't join in. Unlike my sister I was no good in crowds.

Every week like the dutiful daughter I pretended to be I called Daddy to make sure all was well at Ravenswood. He didn't much like extended telephone conversations and would soon hand the phone to Mildred Knapp. She'd lived in the tower ever since Harriet died. She cleaned and cooked for him and Iris thought she did more for him than that. I could see her standing with the phone to her ear and Daddy prompting her. She couldn't speak freely but it hardly mattered. She and I had never been friends. What I did get from her was news of Iris. After graduating from her school upstate, my sister planned to move to the city. The idea of Iris living in New York alarmed me and it must have alarmed Daddy too, and I wasn't surprised when he suggested that she move in with Sidney and me so I could play the maternal role as I had during her teenage years after Harriet died. Sidney was amenable but I was not. Over my dead body, I said.

Fortunately for me, Iris wanted to live downtown and I was spared having to refuse to take her in. Nothing with Iris ever

happened simply. There always had to be drama, emotion, confusion. She'd made several visits to New York while she was in
college and I was never unhappy to put her on a train back upstate.
She was more trouble than she'd ever been in high school. In the
brief periods I'd spent with her she exhausted me. She wasn't
beautiful, not in any conventional sense. Her face was too fat and
her teeth weren't straight although she did have fine dark eyes and
her skin was creamy. She was as tall as me but fleshy. Men certainly
found her attractive.

As for her hair, it was blonde, though not as pale as mine, more
a dirty blonde, and there was too much of it considering how little
maintenance it got. I'd often seen her damp with tears and her hair
glued wetly to her face, such a mess she made of herself. An impossible girl. But within a week of her arrival she'd found a railroad
apartment over a noodle shop in Chinatown. How she got a
Chinese landlord to rent to her I never did discover, everybody
said you had to speak Cantonese to live in Chinatown, although to
be fair it was more the Bowery where she lived. She'd also found
a job in a hotel. Sidney was impressed. Iris amused him and he
approved of her ambition to become a doctor. He believed she'd
make a fine doctor once she was settled. She possessed what he
called a *robust personality*. He said she had *messy vitality*. He meant
she was loud and had appetites, and by *this* he meant she'd acquired
a taste for liquor, also for men. She attracted older men and didn't
care if they were married or not. This I knew because when
installed in some cellar bar in Greenwich Village, where she really
felt at home, over copious cocktails she liked nothing better than
to tell me about her sex life.

I've never been comfortable with frank sexual talk. But Iris liked to indulge herself. With a martini in one hand and a cigarette in the other, her eyes bright and her hair adrift, she mocked my scandalized reactions when she spoke with candor about her affairs. She behaved as though I belonged to a different generation, as in a way I did. She told me I'd married too soon.

—I like Sidney, she said, but New York's full of clever men if that's what you want.

—I've had enough of clever men, I said.

—Enough of them, she cried, oh, Constance, there's never enough of them. There's always more.

—Iris, where did you learn to talk like that?

Meanwhile Sidney decided that we should give a dinner party so we could introduce this messy beatnik floozy to some of our friends. Sidney said she needed friends in the city. I told him Iris was more than capable of finding her own friends. But she was my sister so I agreed. I went to see her after work and told her about the dinner we were planning. She was absurdly pleased.

—No one's ever given a dinner in my honor, she said.

I told her she'd better behave herself. I reminded her what happened at our wedding.

—I was just a kid then.

The evening of the party, the weather was warm and all the windows in the apartment were open. I was dreading it. As our guests began to arrive Sidney mixed a pitcher of martinis. He was smoking a cigar. Ed Kaplan wanted to know where this famous sister of mine was.

—She'll be here very soon, I said.

We were in a large paneled room with a good Persian carpet and a pair of oxblood chesterfields either side of a low table and a fireplace, all very masculine. There was a wall of books with a library ladder on rollers and a drinks table. It got very hot in the summer. The martinis were disappearing swiftly. The guests were talking loudly. Everyone was smoking. Ed Kaplan was putting it around that Iris didn't exist. Better we dine with the idea of Iris, he said, less risk of disappointment. It was all very droll but the guests were getting drunk and still there was no Iris. I drew Sidney aside.

—I'm serving, I said. Get them to the table.

We'd already filed into the dining room and sat down when we heard her at the door. I asked Ed to please let her in. Then we heard her stilettos tapping smartly across the hall floor. She stared with surprise at the assembled company.

—Christ, am I late? she cried hoarsely. Then her eyes grew wide. There was a *fire*, she said.

She was in a low-cut red cocktail dress that clung to her ample figure, and with her blonde thatch piled up on top in a sort of leaky beehive, and in those heels, she stood about six feet tall. She worked her way around the table, bending to shake the hand of each of the guests in turn, and being not withholding with the cleavage. Ellen Taussig, so demure, cast a glance in my direction but Iris was charming when she reached her. She said she'd heard so much about her.

—My dear, said Ellen, was it yourself that caught fire?

Iris stared at her and for a second or two an odd silence filled the dining room. She really was very young. Somewhere in the street a man shouted an obscenity. Then Iris realized that this elegant and dignified woman was making a joke. She lifted her head and loosed off a scream of laughter that sounded to me like nothing so much as a lot of empty bottles being smashed in a fireplace. They all joined in, even Ellen was infected with Iris's laughter. It was kind of hysterical there for a while. What a success she was.

I don't know why I started thinking about Harriet's death that night. It was always painful to remember her last months. I was twelve when she got sick and she wasn't so old after all, she was only thirty-seven. I remember being angry with her and at the same time I knew enough not to show it. I think she understood. Daddy was less able to cope with her illness than I was. He was a doctor. He'd seen cancer before and he knew the end of the story. Cancer is cancer, he once said, and he said it with such cold finality it made me shiver. There was no remission. It was a lump on her lung and she must have been in pain for some time before she told anyone about it. Poor Harriet. She was a stoic, Daddy said. In the eyes of the child I then was she became ethereal; there was little I couldn't romanticize in those days. I tried not to be sad in her presence, that was the hardest thing. But when I was sad I gave her at least the gratification of consoling me. I think she needed that. So I provided her with an opportunity to be useful.

She hated being looked after. When she was in the hospital she seemed smaller and sicker than she ever did at home because at home she had some influence over the household. Mildred Knapp was coming in every day and the pair of them would consult on domestic matters.

The funeral was dreadful. I had charge of Iris or I'd have fallen apart. Daddy fell apart. Back at the house people were milling about. Mildred had made sandwiches. There were drinks. I was very distraught. But the adults seemed to think it was some kind of a cocktail party. At one point I heard one of our neighbors say to another that the poor doctor "didn't know what hit him." I had an extreme reaction to those words. I had to leave the room. There was a bathroom under the front stairs, a dank little lavatory with noisy pipes where I often went to read or just think, with the door locked. I threw up in the toilet. I heard it again: *He didn't know what hit him.* I'd heard it before, perhaps in a dream. I sat there for a long time with my head in my hands.

It passed off soon enough. I recovered, more or less, and life went on. The next time it happened I thought somebody was talking to me but there was nobody in the room. It came as a shock to realize it was in my head. I didn't tell anybody else about it. But I never thought I was going mad. It was just a bad memory.

One night in New York Iris asked me if I remembered the day Harriet died. It wasn't an easy question. I'd boxed up my memories of those last weeks and secured them in a room in my mind I tried never to enter if I could help it. I knew I was watching her die and one time I asked Daddy when it was going to happen. I remember how clinical he was, how very cold.

—A few more days, he said. A very few.

I hadn't realized it would be so soon. It was heartbreaking. You didn't have to be an impressionable young girl of strong imaginative tendency to quaff the brimming cup of pathos in those words! I began to want her suffering to end. I wanted her to die and I felt guilty for wanting it. But how merciful it would be if she slipped away, or if I quietly ended her life for her, just covered her face with a pillow and pressed down hard for five minutes. I was sure that was what she wanted. I hated how thin she'd become, nothing but bones, and her dim, drugged eyes gazing out at me, and always that horrid sweet smell of decay in the room. Her hand like a claw rising from the counterpane, clutching at me when I drew near—

I couldn't say this to Iris. She was like Harriet, she had a big heart. She was an open book. Nobody said she wasn't a proper person. I remember telling her about the sadness of those days, and Daddy saying that death was a good thing if it brought an end to suffering. Just a sort of sleep, he said. Nothing about an afterlife. He was always a godless man.

—You know we all thought she was by herself when she died? said Iris.

I did. There were times when nobody was in the room with her and that was when it happened. Daddy went in a few minutes later and discovered the body. I remember Mildred Knapp telling us in the kitchen later that day as we sat staring into our teacups that she chose to go when she was alone. She said her husband, Walter, went that way. Then she clapped her hand to her mouth.

I never forgot how Mildred's hand flew to her mouth when she said the name of her late husband. Walter. Walter Knapp. She'd never mentioned him before. We hadn't thought of Mildred having a *husband*, sour old Mildred. It made a strong impression on Iris too.

—You get to choose? she whispered.

—Sometimes, said Mildred. If you're lucky.

Harriet's death was in the end a relief but it took Daddy a long time to get over it. I realized later he felt bad that he wasn't with her at the end, to ease the pain of her departure. All this was in my mind as Iris told me she wasn't alone.

—What are you saying?

—I was with her.

I was shocked. She told me she'd gone into the bedroom and Harriet was gasping as though she couldn't get enough air in her lungs. Iris thought she should go get Daddy but Harriet wanted her to stay with her. So Iris got in bed with her and held her hand. Then she died.

—How did you know?

—Her fingers went limp and it got real quiet.

—What did you do?

—After a bit I went away.

—Why didn't you tell anyone?

—I thought I'd get in trouble.

We stared at each other for a second. Then we burst out laughing. How we howled, oh, gales of mirth. We couldn't help it. Iris had never told anybody until she told me, that's how close we were. But at the same time I felt resentful. It was I who should have been with her at the end.

★

So after Iris had her great success at the dinner Sidney gave in her honor I asked her please to show me the hotel where she worked. I was trying to look out for her. This was what Harriet had wanted

13

me to do, for all I knew it was a mother's dying wish. It was dusk and we were standing on the sidewalk in front of a brownstone on the corner of West Thirty-third not far from Penn Station. In the sky over Jersey I glimpsed a few smears of rusty sunset. There were black clouds overhead. I felt uneasy. The last of the light burnished the windows of the tenements opposite and made the fire escapes gleam. There was an empty lot just down the block with a chain-link fence around it. Some young men stood around, aimless and smoking. They kept looking at us. I didn't like it. Iris told me it wasn't so bad inside.

—You don't say.

Wide stone steps with brass handrails ascended to a door over-hung by a canopy embossed with the hotel's crest. Pigeons roosted on the ledge above. As we mounted the steps they fluttered off into the gloom. We were greeted by a black man in a frayed gray uniform with scarlet piping. He welcomed us to the Dunmore Hotel. He greeted Iris by name.

—Hi, Simon, she said, this is my big sis.

She then took from her purse a pair of spectacles with heavy black frames and put them on. They transformed her completely. She looked like an intellectual!

—Don't look at me like that, she said, I need them.

We entered a lobby with a tiled floor and pots of dusty ferns. Old leather armchairs and couches were grouped around low tables. The place was shabby, but a vestige of gentility still clung to it, and I imagined lonely salesmen checking in with their suitcases full of samples, then slipping out to buy a mickey of rye or what-ever. By the reception desk a broad carpeted staircase ascended to the floors above. I discovered then, for I heard him, that the Dunmore boasted a pianist. Apparently he performed nightly in the cocktail lounge. His name was Eddie Castrol and Iris was eager that I meet him. I wanted to know why.

—Are you going to get mad at me?

—It depends what you're going to say.

Already my heart was sinking. Then she was telling me that she'd gotten involved with this man. That was why she wanted me to meet him. I told her I was going straight home unless she told me who he was. I was very firm about it. So we sat in the lobby for half an hour and she told me that this time it was the real thing.

—Oh, is it? I said.

She led me through to the lounge. It was a large gloomy room with scattered tables, a small dance floor, and a bar. The few customers sat alone or in huddled whispering couples. Lamps in scalloped shades gave out a muted yellowy glow. The atmosphere was strange and sad and vaguely dreamlike, and made more so by the presence of a man in a shabby tuxedo sitting at a concert grand on the far side of the room. A cigarette hung from the corner of his mouth. He was playing something I couldn't identify. It was oddly disconnected, spiky somehow. *Syncopated.* I am acutely sensitive to music. I am acutely sensitive to all sound.

—Doesn't he remind you of Daddy? whispered Iris.

He did not! It was alarming that Iris should think he did. She showed me to a booth, then signaled the waitress and stood a moment gazing at Eddie Castrol through her ridiculous spectacles. He was grinning at us now. Iris walked off. I ordered a martini. Again I looked over at this man who reminded my sister of Daddy.

His skin was like parchment, bleached white in the spotlight's glare, but he could play piano all right.

He was aware of my eyes on him. He leaned forward, head down, cigarette between his lips, poking at the keys like a bird digging worms, and shifted into of all things *Moon River*. Nobody else was listening. He played it very slow and moody. Too sentimental for me.

I drifted into a reverie. I saw my sister in the arms of this lizardy man. I imagined him feasting on her plump soft heavy body like some kind of animal. It was a disquieting thought. He ended the set before she came back and with some abruptness stood up from the piano and crossed the room to thin applause. He had my full attention now. I lit a cigarette, it was that kind of a night. He slid smoothly into the booth beside me and introduced himself. He then turned toward the bar.

—Where's that girl gone now?

It was the waitress he wanted. He grinned at me over his cigarette. He then made short work of a large gin and called for another. Lush, I thought. He swallowed gin like it was water. He leaned in and confided that he wouldn't be here if the money wasn't so good.

I turned away.

—Don't embarrass me, I said.

I was cold to him. I had nothing but disdain for this seedy man and this crummy joint my sister worked in. If it hadn't been for her I'd have walked out. He lifted his hands as though to say: So what are we to talk about? And I thought: Yes, what *are* we to talk about?

—Iris told me you write music.

I was making conversation, nothing more. He pursed his lips as though he were about to kiss something and gazed at his gin with lifted eyebrows. Was it such a complicated question?

—Yeah, I write stuff, he said at last.

—*Stuff?* I said. I reached for another cigarette. I was not at ease. I suspected that the jagged thing he'd been playing when I came in was his stuff. I edit stuff, I said, stuff that others write. You think your stuff's like my stuff or is my stuff different stuff?

He lit my cigarette then dropped his eyes but there it was, I saw it again, that bent grin of his. I'd amused him. I hadn't meant to, but I was gratified all the same.

—You want to talk about it? I said.

He was from Miami. His father introduced him to chamber music when he was seven years old. He'd gotten into the Juilliard School but he didn't last long. I asked him why and he said he could go faster on his own. I laughed a little. I didn't believe a word of it.

—So tell me something, I said.

—Sure.

—What are you doing in this dump?

I caught him by surprise. I got a bark of laughter out of him. He laid his hands flat on the table. He had the thinnest, most spidery fingers I'd ever seen, yellow at the tips. Perhaps that's why he reminded Iris of Daddy.

—Dump is right. I'm only here for your sister.

He knew it wasn't true and so did I. He needed the money, pitiful though it surely was. But I played along.

17

—You'd do that for Iris? She's only here for you.

—She thinks we have a future.

He gazed straight at me as he lit another cigarette.

—Don't you?

—Oh, come on, baby. You know my situation.

—I know you're married. Baby.

He wasn't abashed at all. Clearly he'd decided there was no point being anything other than straight with me. He drank off his gin and leaned in toward me and there was something of the shark in his expression now.

—And you? he said.

He had both elbows on the table. He was grinning. My glass was empty. He was a lanky loose-jointed man and his hair was oily. There were webs of tiny lines spreading across his cheekbones from the corners of his narrow black eyes. I looked around for the waitress, also for Iris returning. I'd forgotten about her. I felt a little sick. I told him that yes, I was married.

—Going good? he said.

—Mind your own business.

He barked again then stood up from the table and a tension eased that I'd barely been aware of. Later we went to another bar. That night I was their audience. Some pair they made, him in his old tuxedo and her in that secondhand cocktail dress with her breasts spilling out and a cheap fur slung round her shoulders. Arm in arm we strutted the streets of Greenwich Village, three swells on a bender. Harriet would have been proud.

When I talked to Iris the next day she didn't mention the last part of the evening. The place we'd gone to was hot and smoky. There was jazz. Sometime after midnight Iris and I were settled on bar stools, Eddie Castrol between us with his jacket off, his shirt unbuttoned, and his back to the counter, the perpetual cigarette hanging from his lips. He was damp in places with perspiration. He seemed to know everyone. They all came by to say hi and slap his hand. I asked Iris how she saw their future. I should have known better.

—Eddie? she said.

—Lover.

—My sister wants to know what your intentions are. You want to call the whole thing off?

She spread a hand across her chest and sang the line in a deep wavering tuneless bass register: *But ooooh, if we call the whole thing off, then we must part—*

Eddie pulled her to him, spilling gin on her dress, but she didn't care. She was happy as a child to be handled by this long-fingered piano player from Miami: He reminded her of Daddy. She laid her head on his shoulder, one arm hanging free as he stroked her hair then kissed it. She lifted her face and he kissed her on the lips. He was watching me while he did it. My prediction: She'd wind up with a broken heart. She was a good kid to hang around with but she was still a kid. He was too old for her. Too old, too jaundiced. Too married.

I went back to the Dunmore a few nights later. I didn't tell Iris I was doing this, I knew how it would look, the adults conferring about her welfare behind her back. She'd be furious. And this was the second time. When I walked in he saw me at once. He played a few bars of *Moon River* then joined me in the booth. He said to what did he owe the honor this time, and I said I wanted to thank him. He knew what I meant.

—How is she?

—She's suffering now, I said. She'll get over it. What did you tell her?

He'd told her what I'd suggested he tell her. That was a few days earlier. I'd gone to the hotel and made it clear to him that he had to leave Iris alone. I said she was very young and he'd only do her harm. He didn't protest. Then we'd talked about his family. We'd parted on good terms.

Now he was frowning at the table and tapping the rim of his glass. He gazed at me and shook his head.

—What is it? I said.

Then he had an elbow on the table, his fingers splayed across his forehead. The lounge was busy that night. Women stopped by the table to say hello. He was charming to every one of them.

—Ah, lord, he said.

—Don't tell me you love her, I said.

—Do I love her? he said.

He lifted his suffering eyes to mine. What a performer he was. Then all at once his mood lifted. The clouds parted, he leaned in. He touched my hand. Now he was tender.

—It'd be different, he said, but there's the kid to think of.

—Kids survive divorce.

—Not my Francie.

I had to excuse myself and go to the ladies' room, where I sat in a stall until I felt quiet again. *Kids survive divorce.* Did Sidney's kid survive his divorce?

★

It was at around this time he came home from visiting his ex-wife in New Jersey and told me he had a serious favor to ask me. I was working at the kitchen table that day. I was engaged in the edit of a badly written manuscript from which I was deriving no joy but Ellen Taussig had asked me to do it, it was a special job. He wanted to know if I'd mind if Howard stayed with us for a few days. The mother was going into the hospital. I asked him what was expected of me.

—Just be civil.

Gladys would cook his meals and as he was a quiet child he wouldn't trouble me in the evenings. We'd barely be aware he was in the apartment. Sidney didn't know where else he could go.

So the next day I came home to find a thin, solemn boy sitting in Sidney's kitchen with a plate of hot dogs in front of him. A curtain of hair the color of pale straw fell over his forehead, his arms and legs were like jointed sticks, and he had the fingers of a violinist. I guess my head was full of musicians then. He bore little resemblance to Sidney, who was a large heavy man of florid complexion and diminutive hands and feet.

He stood up when I walked into the kitchen, and I thought, Why, he's a little gentleman.

—Hello, Howard Klein, I said.

—Hello, Mrs. Klein.

—Sit down, I said. Don't you want mustard on those?

—No, thank you.

—Ketchup?

—No, thank you.

He sat down and I realized he wouldn't be a problem. I remember thinking I was just like Howard at that age, scrupulously polite so as to guard my inner life from the adults. So the next day I suggested to Sidney that we get out of the city. He was busy with his book. He hated to be interrupted. I told him it wasn't for myself that I asked, I thought Howard would like it.

—You're right, he said. We could go visit your father.

—That's not what I had in mind.

I'd had enough of Daddy. We'd spent Labor Day with him. Instead we drove out to Long Island and spent the weekend in Montauk. It was good to get away. It was too cold to swim in the ocean but we took long windy walks on the beach. There were dunes, and driftwood, and heaps of large flat stones, and big shiny clumps of seaweed swept in on the autumn tides. I watched Howard and his father kneeling on the damp sand to inspect a dead sea turtle. Sidney turned it over with a stick and Howard shrieked with joy when dozens of tiny black crabs came swarming out. We had dinner in a seafood shack. The wind had put color in Howard's face, dabs of red high on his cheeks, and it had done the same to me. Sidney was pleased. He wanted us to be friends, Howard and I. He thought it would be good for me. It would get my mind off my father, he said, if I had to behave like a mother.

One night around this time I had to get myself all fixed up for a faculty party of Sidney's that I didn't want to attend. I was in the bedroom. I wanted to wear my gray silk thing. Sidney came in looking for his watch. He was concerned about the time. I didn't feel like being nice to him. He hadn't been sympathetic when I told him that Iris had had her heart broken and was very depressed. He said it was simple. She should stop drinking and go into analysis.

—You're making me nervous, I said. Can't you go read the paper or something?

I watched him in the mirror. He sat on the bed and stared at his hands and frowned. I was pressing tissues to my face so it would stay matte in the heat.

I selected a lipstick. Poor Iris. That morning I'd visited her. I hated how she lived now. Her apartment was on the third floor of a tenement just south of the Manhattan Bridge. When I stepped into the lobby the smell of boiled vegetables almost made me sick. I climbed the three flights and found her door already open. She shouted at me to come in. The place was a shambles. She tried to keep it in some sort of order but she wasn't a tidy girl and she'd been up all night. I heard the shower come on. I stood at the window and looked down at the street below. There were Chinese people scurrying along the sidewalk and bums sitting under the statue of Confucius. They were passing bottles in brown paper bags. The traffic was loud so I closed the window. Almost at once the tiny apartment became close and sticky. It was a dank, dull day in the fall and the sky was threatening rain.

She appeared in her bathrobe toweling her hair. She apologized for the state of the apartment. She'd been planning a big houseclean yesterday but she'd been called out to do a little *hostessing*, whatever that meant. She got a couple of cold beers out of the icebox and yawned while she looked for clean glasses. I no longer tried telling her she was made for better things. Then we were sitting at a low table heaped with lurid novels and cheap magazines and medical journals, also a half-empty bottle of brandy, cheap Spanish stuff. After the breakup with Eddie they'd had a few last trysts in the hotel but now that was all over too and she was again foundering.

—What the hell am I going to do? she said.

I was very clear about this. I took her hands in mine and spoke firmly to her.

—You're going to study medicine and work very hard and forget all about Eddie and become a doctor. That's what you're going to do.

She turned away. I'd aroused not even a flicker of resolve in her.

—I've got a bad feeling about it, she said.

—What do you mean?

—I don't think I want to do medicine.

—Oh, for Christ's sake. Don't even talk like that. You have to, for Daddy's sake.

I got impatient with her. She'd been able to laugh at herself once. Now she was so damn sulky all the time. When a thing's over it's over, I said. What was wrong with her? She began to grope in her purse. She fetched out her cigarettes and a lighter. I suggested we take a walk. I wanted to get her out of the building, it was unpleasantly warm and there was too much noise. Without a word she stood up and went into her bedroom to get dressed.

We walked east. The weather remained oppressive. Down by the Brooklyn Bridge the streets were deserted. The silence was a relief. There were a few pigeons around but no other signs of life.

Half the buildings on Beekman were boarded up. The whole neighborhood was being demolished, warehouses, printing establishments, liquor stores, barber shops. Where the rubble had been trucked away tracts of wasteland strewn with lumps of concrete stretched for blocks. It didn't improve Iris's mood but I got a kind of satisfaction from seeing a whole section of the city disappearing as though it had been H-bombed, and I felt the same about Penn Station, which was also coming down. I passed through it whenever I took the train upstate. They were turning it into a ruin. I liked ruins. I'd grown up in one, of course. Sweep away the old stuff, this was my feeling. Start over! Build it new! Then it began to rain. We were out front of a warehouse on William Street with no door.

We climbed the narrow staircase. The paint was flaking off the wall. One floor up the stairs opened into an empty loft with exposed brick painted white. Old iron radiators stood amid the trash and at the far end empty window frames looked south to the Wall Street skyscrapers. There was a picture of Marilyn Monroe taped to the brick and beneath it a rickety wooden chair. Iris sat down and lit a cigarette. The rain continued heavy. She stared at the floor and I saw a tear fall. She looked up, wiping her face. At times she seemed so young I was moved by her predicament. But mostly I just got impatient with her.

—I don't know if I'll survive this, she said.

—Are you serious?

—I've never loved anyone like this before. I'd better get used to it.

—To what?

—Being incomplete.

25

I cleared a space on the floor and sat down beside her.

—Oh, honey, I said, you'll get over it, what are you, twenty-two?

She turned on me.

—Constance, will you just *shut the fuck up?*

I guess it was a thoughtless thing to say. The wound was too fresh or something. I apologized.

—It's okay. But you don't have to reassure me. I hate being reassured.

I asked her why she wouldn't get over him.

—We never got to the end. It was still growing. It would have gone on growing a long time. So it's this unfinished thing in me.

I'd never heard love described like this before. As a growing thing, I mean, like a tree. So it comes to life, it grows to maturity, then what, death? It had never happened to me that way. A little later she asked me if I thought he saw a shrink.

—No.

—Why do you say that?

—I just don't think he does.

—But why? He said he didn't but I don't believe it. Everyone in New York sees a shrink except me.

—He's from Miami. He's a piano player. He's a lush. Honey, I don't know, I just don't think he does.

She didn't want to hear the truth but at the same time candor was what she said she wanted.

—What are you doing tonight? she said.

—Some party Sidney wants to go to.

—Come out with me. It doesn't matter about the party.

—It does to Sidney.

—Constance, please.

—Why is it a problem?

—I'm afraid I'll lose you.

—Don't be absurd. Iris, this is madness!

She stood up. She walked to the window and with her hands on the sill she leaned out. I was suddenly afraid for her. I'd never seen her like this. It wasn't just the man. I told her to come away from the window. She said the rain had stopped. We could go.

We walked east to the seaport. The day was brighter now. The sun was breaking through. The stink of fish from the Fulton Street market made me feel nauseous. Iris suggested a cocktail.

—It's not even twelve o'clock, I said.

—Just one.

We sat at a table in an empty bar on South Street. I'd never known her to drink liquor in the middle of the day and it didn't make me feel any easier about her. When she decided to have another one I had to speak up.

—Won't you need a clear head later?

—No.

—Why not?

—The work I do, you think they care?

When the affair with Eddie ended she'd quit her job at the hotel and joined an agency that supplied hostesses to nightclubs. They gave her three nights a week. It was enough to sustain life, she said. She didn't have many overheads.

—Isn't that the truth. But I'm worried about you.

It was true. I *was* worried. I didn't believe Iris could be brought so low by a man—and a man like that! She laughed but it was hollow. As though she'd stopped caring what happened to her.

—It's not as though anyone gives a damn, she said.

—I do.

She said nothing. Suddenly I felt not that she was losing me but that I was losing her. I didn't know what was going on. I'd assumed she was more resilient than this. She'd gone to the counter to get her scotch, and in the gloom of the place she was consumed by shadows and I couldn't see her properly. I felt like she was drifting out to sea—

★

You want a drink? said Sidney.

I was rudely jolted from my somber thoughts.

—Not yet. And I don't think you should have one either.

I was still angry with him. I think I was also guilty about Iris and taking it out on him. But what was I, some kind of alcohol cop now?

—Sidney, sweetheart, please go away.

I finished with my eyes then slipped off the bathrobe and examined myself in the long mirror. I may have been a few years older than Iris but you wouldn't know it. Sidney used to say I had a boy's body, these days he'd prefer it if I was a boy, I wasn't much use to him as a girl. I opened my underwear drawer and fingered my silky things. There was a tune in my head, *Moon River. Moon River.* It had been troubling me for days.

The party was an anticlimax. A man Sidney wanted to meet who'd written a book didn't show and he was irritated. He was also mad at me about something I'd said. I freely admit I'd been less than sweetly charming all night but hell, it was an uptown crowd of professors and they weren't interested in me, some mere editorial person.

When we got home I said so and next thing we were arguing, never a good idea after a few drinks. We went back and forth for a while and then I left the room. I wanted a cigarette but where could I get one now? I became aware of movement down the hallway. Standing in his pajamas gazing at me in the dim glow of the night-light was Howard. He was a restless sleeper like me. Swiftly I went to him.

—What are you doing?

—You woke me up.

I took his hand and led him back into his bedroom.

—I'm so sorry, I whispered. Let's get you back in bed, shall we?

I sat him down on the bed and he wriggled in under the sheet. He turned on his side and gazed up at me.

—Were you and Papa fighting?

—Just talking loud. Go to sleep now.

—Talking loud, he murmured, and fell asleep.

I sat beside him on the bed for a few minutes. When I left him I met Sidney in the hallway.

—He asleep? he said.

I nodded. I put my arms round him. He was surprised. I asked him to hold me. Tentatively at first, then with more conviction, he held me. I felt quiet now. His presence sometimes had this effect. I lay my cheek on his shoulder. He began to stroke my hair. Then he lifted my chin and took my face in his fingers and kissed me. He steered me toward the bedroom. Once, we'd resolved all our quarrels in bed. When we were inside he kicked the door shut. He pushed me down on the bed. He began to undress me. I sat up. I wasn't sure I wanted this.

—Sidney—

—Don't talk.

He watched me closely as he stepped out of his trousers. Then he was lying beside me on the bed.

—Just wait, I whispered, I'm not ready. All right, that's better. Now you can.

Times like that I loved him but they were rare.

★

I went by Iris's apartment again the next day. I wanted to know if she'd thought any more about medical school. Her eyes were red and her hair was lank and sweaty: two bad nights and she looked like death. She told me that more and more she was losing the thread and drifting into the past.

—Oh, honey.

I didn't find it easy to contain my irritation. Distinct scenes presented as though from some ill-remembered movie, she said, and it was the passion of those days that roused such anguish in her. But then she was telling me she wasn't the woman she'd been when she first met him. You laugh, Constance, she said, but it's true: I've changed. I've grown up. I can love that man now, and the irony is I won't be given a chance even though he needs me—

This was Iris, clinging to a fraying thread of hope, sustaining the belief that the man wasn't lost to her forever. I thought about it in the subway going home, crowded between men in thin ties and bad-tempered women exhausted from fending them off. But of course he was lost to her. She would never get him back now. She was drinking heavily, often alone, and I suspected her life had gone off the rails in ways she wasn't telling me about. And her response when I'd asked her what this "hostessing" involved!

—It's just looking after men.

—What do you mean?

—They have to have a good time. Spend money.

—On you?

—Sure, on me! What is this, the third degree? You think I have sex with them?

—Do you?

She gave me a look I found hard to read. I knew what it wasn't, it wasn't an outraged negative.

—Iris, are you *whoring?*

—Very funny.

I left her in good spirits, halfway drunk at five in the afternoon. I thought, New York's going to destroy that girl if she's not careful.

Later with Gladys's help I made supper for Howard. He was sitting quietly at the kitchen table. Then he looked up and made his solemn announcement.

—Constance and Papa weren't fighting last night. They were just talking loud.

Gladys was amused. What an odd little boy he was. I was growing fond of him.

—That's right, Howard, I said. We were just talking loud.

TWO

THE DAY THEY started tearing down the old Penn Station I heard from my lawyer, Ed Kaplan, that the divorce from Barb had gone through. Ed commiserated. Sidney, he said, it's nobody's fault. I didn't believe him. It wasn't nobody's fault, I said, there'd been love when we started, what happened to it? I let it die. My son Howard, age six, was living with his mother in New Jersey and I was supposed to be relieved that a bad and worsening marital situation had come to an end? I wasn't. All I saw was failure.

Now we were divorced. I wandered from room to room and grew disconsolate at the unfamiliar silence. I'd held on to the apartment because Barb didn't want it. She wanted to be in Atlantic City with her family. Her brother Gerry Mulcahy managed a small casino there.

—It's not the other side of the world, she said.

—It's far enough. When will I ever see my son?

—Whenever you want.

Barb did the accounting for the casino and I only discovered much later how ill she was. I was aware of her fatigue each time I drove out to New Jersey to take Howard for the afternoon. I attributed it to the tedium of her job and the awfulness of living in Atlantic City among members of her own family. They weren't an inspiring outfit but they were friendly enough to me. They called me "the professor." I knew that if I'd been able to sustain the marriage, Barb's life wouldn't have been half so miserable as it turned out, and I said this to her on one of my visits. She was renting a place a block from her mother's house. Howard was in the yard, I could see him out there on his hands and knees. He was interested in snails at the time. She'd leaned across the table and touched my cheek.

—Sidney, she'd said, it's not your fault, but thanks for the thought.

What went wrong? She was a good-looking woman and we'd liked each other well enough once. Then out of the blue she decided that I wasn't giving her what she needed, and that what I did give her she didn't want. Resentment broke out, and once that happens the sex life goes all to hell and soon the marriage was wrecked beyond repair. It was all too depressing to contemplate. I'm with Goethe on the correct response to a failing marriage. Resignation. The preservation of order at all costs. Stoic nobility of spirit. But I wasn't allowed to suffer with stoic nobility of spirit, instead Barb moved out, taking Howard with her, and that's why I had the place to myself. It was on West Sixty-ninth, a few blocks from Central Park. There was no shortage of bookshelves, all of which I'd filled, and numerous rooms including an airless spare bedroom that gave off the kitchen. But it was too big for one man, and there was a problem with the boiler in the basement. The super couldn't control it. In winter the pipes in the walls got so hot it was like living in a steam bath. If I opened a window I got a blast of frigid air. So I either baked or froze, like some kind of a reptile. A large English crocodile perhaps.

I was too restless to read and it was too late to do any writing, and anyway I'd had a drink. So I went to bed at half past nine with a couple of scholarly journals and that day's newspaper. The neighborhood got noisy around ten. In those days there was always shouting at night, sometimes screaming, only on rare occasions gunshots. Then I'd hear the sirens of approaching cop cars, or I wouldn't. Often they just didn't show. What was happening was this. The city had started to show symptoms of the sickness that would rip it apart and leave us unable to heal ourselves, or police ourselves, even *pay* for ourselves. New York was remaking itself, but into what? Barb believed no marriage could survive in a city like that. It was another bad theory of breakdown in my opinion. Nobody's fault, contingent circumstances: all excuses. Why did nobody take responsibility?

As for Penn Station, apparently there was no money in railroads anymore. Interstate highways and airplanes had done them in. Anyway it had been deteriorating for decades. It was neglected and begrimed, it took up two entire city blocks, and in New York it just made no economic sense, unless you believed that a railroad station possessing all the solemn grandeur of a Gothic cathedral was worth preserving for its own sake. It broke my heart to see the demolition crew arrive with their jackhammers that drizzly morning in October, the day I got divorced for the *second* time.

Three years it took them to strip it down to a skeletal structure of steel girders and dump its columns and statuary in the New Jersey Meadowlands, where you could see it from the Philadelphia train and weep. I wept. All this with no interruption in service, which New Yorkers soon took for granted, oblivious to the staggering acts of vandalism going on around them—

Forgive me. I feel about architecture as I do about marriage. What was done to Penn Station was wanton. I hate to see a thing destroyed before its time. I tried to stay busy. I was writing a book called *The Conservative Heart* and lecturing at one of the city colleges, which at least got me out of the building and provided what social life I required. When I received invitations to faculty parties and other functions I tossed them in the trash.

Months passed, gloomy, solitary months for me. *My spirit walked not with the souls of men.* Fall turned to winter, winter to spring. The pipes in the apartment cooled down but the city itself became unendurable as the temperature started to rise, also the tempers of my restive fellow citizens. Meanwhile *The Conservative Heart* advanced fitfully. One day it was brilliant, the next it stank. The problem was this. I was known to be a brilliant lecturer. What was so hard to communicate on paper was the excitement I aroused when I spoke to a packed lecture hall. I was often swept away when an idea caught fire in my mind, and more was taught then than could ever be expressed in sober prose. Often I despaired as I struggled to articulate, oh, the apparent paradox of romantic conservatism, or the seven principles of inspiration as I'd first formulated them in my post-doctoral work at Oxford.

I missed talking to Barb about it. How do writers alone survive? What had once been unimaginable was now my reality. But I got used to it, the absence of a domesticity that once had irritated me but that now I missed. I drove down to Atlantic City to see Howard whenever I could. Barb and I behaved in front of him with stiff formality at first, but later with more warmth. She wasn't looking well and I guess I wasn't either. I told her I'd arrived at no startling thesis regarding marriage and its discontents, but privately I'd decided that my own recent performance unfitted me for further service. I shared these thoughts with Ed Kaplan. He'd come by to commiserate some more.

Ed practiced criminal law but he'd handled the divorce as a personal favor. He was fascinated by the new condition of life he found me in. To live alone in the unmarried state was to Ed an extraordinary thing. As it was to me. He said he didn't get it. He was married to a lovely dark creature called Naomi and they lived down the block with their four daughters, whom they were appar-ently raising as anarchists. He liked to ask me what my plans were. What did I intend to do with myself now?

—Work.

—Just work? All work? No play?

—No play.

—Sidney, trust me, you're not made for this. You need a woman. You better get out there and see what's around.

—Ed, for Christ's sake. No woman wants me now.

—You don't know that until you meet her. You think you'll never marry again?

—That's what I do think.

—You're an idiot.

I didn't believe him. He left a little later. The apartment was once again as quiet as the grave, apart from the sirens and the screaming and the rest. But he'd unsettled me. A few mornings later an invitation came in the mail. It was to a book party in a townhouse on Sutton Place, I forget whose townhouse and I forget whose book, I even forget why I went unless I sensed it was Destiny Calling. It doesn't matter now but what I *don't* forget is the first glimpse I had of a tall blonde girl in a narrow black skirt, thin as a pencil, no makeup, with long legs and a pursed, tight little mouth. She was standing by an open window with a martini in her hand, silent and aloof amid the shrieking hubbub of civilized conversation all around her. Her lips were moving slightly.

She's told me often enough that when she saw me pushing through the crowd in her direction she looked for the means of escape but there was none. What she remembered most clearly, she said, was my damp mouth and my pink bow tie. I was apparently nodding my head at her as I eased through the throng, as though to say *You, yes you, it's you I want.*

—Sidney Klein, I said, when at last I stood before her.

—You're English.

—I'm afraid so.

So it started. We shook hands. I still can't explain why I felt such an immediate attraction to this young woman unless it was carnal. But there was an air of angry untouchability about her that interested me considerably, and which I assumed concealed fearful bewilderment and naïvété, it's often the mask worn by girls new to the city. And there was something else too, a kind of fineness not at once obvious, and although to the casual glance she might appear to be a plain girl, that fineness was a powerful attractor and I just wanted to get physically close to her. I never lost the feeling.

What she saw in me was less flattering. I am a tall man, perhaps a little on the heavy side, but I dress well. I should also tell you that I am a sentimental man. I feel too much, I always have. It is no accident that I am an authority on Romantic poetry. It was a warm evening. I was in my light seersucker and apparently there were beads of sweat on my forehead. The effect, she said later, was that of an obscure consular official going quietly mad in a far-flung outpost of empire. But there was, too, without question, she said, some force of personality there. She also said I was panting in the heat like a dog.

I suggested we go somewhere quiet where we could talk. She asked me what I wanted to talk about and I said I wanted to talk about her. Why? Why not? We both knew she was about to leave the party with me. When we were out on the street I proposed a quiet French restaurant in the Village. Then we were in the back of a checker cab and I kissed her and she let me, she wanted me to, she liked me, I was so much older than her, at least forty, she thought, and she felt that with me she'd be safe. I only wish I'd kept her safer. I should have kept her under lock and key.

When I kissed her I held her cheek and chin in my fingers. Her skin was like a child's and her lips were soft and cool although they wouldn't part for me. I felt her body stiffen in involuntary protest at first but I paid no attention to that and after a moment she relaxed, and draped a long thin arm around my neck, and briefly kissed me back, but again without involvement of the tongue. For that I'd have to wait. Then she disengaged herself and stared out the window of the cab.

At dinner we talked, as I said we would, about her. I figured her to be about twenty-three. But for some reason she sustained the chilly hauteur I'd seen at the party and I soon began to feel she had no right to it, not having earned it. I persevered, however, still bewitched, or fired up at least with strong emotions loosely rooted in lust. Then as we lingered over our coffee and cigarettes she at last started to open up. I don't know why. Perhaps she took pity on me. Or perhaps she thought I was harmless. I'd asked her about her childhood, and she told me she'd grown up with her sister, Iris, in a falling-down house in the Hudson Valley complete with a framed verandah and a tower. It had been in her family for generations, she said, but when I asked her how many generations she was vague. Oh, two at least, she said. Daddy grew up there. It stood high on a fissured bluff, and on the south side of the property a steep wooded slope descended to a wetland meadow by the railroad tracks and the river. This was the view she'd had from her bedroom window, she said, the sweep of the mighty Hudson far below her, with the Catskills in the distance. It was called Ravenswood.

It was all too good to be true. The old house with its tower on a bluff above the river, and this beautiful girl, clearly in flight from who knows what horrors she'd suffered there, it was a Romantic cliché, the whole thing. But for that I liked it all the more. In fact I hadn't spent much time in the Hudson Valley. There was nothing up there apart from a few small liberal arts colleges, none of them of any interest to me. But this I kept to myself. It hadn't escaped me that this girl got dreamy when she talked about Nature.

She then produced a photograph and pushed it across the table. It was herself aged twelve sitting with her sister on the porch of that old house, which was as she'd described it and every bit as shabby as I'd imagined. It had a long porch, a tower, several steep gables, and what looked like a screened verandah, a kind of American villa with Gothic additions, and pretty run-down. And there she was in the foreground, clutching her school books and frowning at the camera, visibly nervous, her hair pinned up and her slim legs pressed tight together at the knees but splayed at the ankles. She wore white socks and brown sandals with a buckled strap. What a geek, she said as I studied the photo. I said I was sure she grew out of the awkward stage, all children do, but she said she didn't, not for a long time. Had she yet, I thought.

But Iris, the younger sister, looked like trouble even then: a tooth missing, hair all adrift, scabby knees, a true hoyden in the making, and those eyes!—even in that creased black-and-white photo there was no escaping those big dark liquid pools of shining life. Behind the two girls stood an eccentric-looking woman in faded corduroy trousers and a man's shirt, and an old straw hat, and a trug, with a cigarette between her teeth, and I thought at once: English. I knew the type. And behind her, in the shadow of the doorway, a tall indistinct figure who reminded me of the pitchfork man in Grant Wood's *American Gothic*. As I slid the photograph back across the table she told me, as though in answer to a question I hadn't asked, that she wasn't an extrovert like Iris but she didn't believe she was *frail*, psychologically. She was a solitary, yes, and Harriet—this was the mother— hadn't tried to make her otherwise—she hadn't tried to make her anything—but she *had* encouraged her to love her little sister and always look out for her. In this way she'd helped create a bond between the sisters that was supposed to never come undone.

Oh, she'd begun to talk now. The floodgates were opening, and I advanced with care.

—Your mother looks like an interesting woman, I said.

—Harriet's dead.

She lifted her head and stared at me as though to have me look upon her suffering and tremble. Her mother always wanted to be called by her first name, she told me, not *Mommy* or *Mom*.

—How old were you?

—Twelve. Iris takes after her. I don't know who I take after. Not Daddy, that's for sure.

She said this with a fierce light in her eyes and an angry little laugh: *Not Daddy, that's for sure.* Oh ho, Daddy's a problem. Then she said it was her mother's presence in the house that gave the place a sense of home. A child takes this for granted, she said, that the mother's the living heart of the home. It was all lost when Harriet died. This was said dispassionately, carelessly, but the child's grief was not hard to detect. What's happened to this girl, I thought. Why has nobody looked after her?

As for the father, Morgan Schuyler, the doctor, she had no difficulty describing him: a terrible, lank, tousled, frowning man in a baggy gray suit with wide suspenders and big dusty brogues on his feet, and long clever fingers stained yellow at the tips by nicotine—

She shivered, describing this monster. A house like that, there had to be a wicked father figure. The restaurant was almost empty but I wasn't calling for the check just yet. The waiters stood by the end of the counter in long white aprons, talking quietly. The bartender was polishing glasses. It was pleasant to be there at that hour. It was *intime*. I sometimes thought New York did Europe better than Europe did Europe.

—Go on, I said.

—In he'd come, she said, her eyes on the table and her voice low and dramatic—and Harriet would at once be on the alert. I wasn't disturbed by it, not at the time. I'd watch him sit down and rub his face, then he might raise his head and gaze at her with lifted eyebrows, as though to say: Tell me something that doesn't involve an ulcer, or a tumor, or an *inflamed bowel*. Tell me something about *life!*

A pause here. She was running a fingernail down the seam of the tablecloth, smiling to herself. I think she was amused by the inflamed bowel.

—Go on. He wanted to be told something about life.

—Oh, but some days he'd stand at the window and Harriet would catch my eye and put a finger to her lips, and he'd just stare

43

out at the river and his back was all we'd have of him until it abated, I guess it was tension from some decision he'd made about one of his patients and he didn't know if he'd done the right thing. I'd heard him talk like that, I heard it through the door of the sitting room, or from outside on the verandah, when I'd creep under the window so they couldn't see me. Then I'd hear those soft murmuring noises I knew from when I woke up in the night and Harriet came into my bedroom—

Another pause. She could be histrionic, this girl, and she was barely conscious of the impression she made. She was engaged exclusively with her own experience. She frowned, as though she was trying to undo some sort of tricky mental knot. A lick or two of that fine blonde hair had worked free and she brushed it back impatiently. I offered her a cigarette and she took it. Then she stared straight at me and spoke as though she were delivering a shattering revelation.

—Or she didn't! There was no knowing! She might ignore me, and sometimes I thought she wasn't my mother at all, and I was just some girl Daddy found in a ditch and brought home for his wife to look after! You think that's silly. You think I'm exaggerating. You think I'm a fool.

—I don't think you're a fool.

Quieter now, smoking her cigarette, she turned slightly in her chair to cross her legs and give me her three-quarter profile. She said she'd often heard voices raised in anger in the sitting room, and then her mother weeping, after which her father stormed out and the door slammed. When that happened she knew to keep out of their way.

—Where was your sister in all this?

She became guarded now. She briefly closed her eyes.

—Iris is younger than me. She's my kid sister. She wants to be me. She'd like me to die and get out of her way. She's always been much better with Daddy. She knows how to talk to him about his work. I always thought this was the problem between us, I mean me and Daddy, my indifference to medicine. He's always wanted one of us to be a doctor and I've made it clear *it's not going to be me!*

She glanced at me to see if I was impressed with her independence of spirit. I was more impressed, or astonished rather, by her frank revelation of primal sibling rivalry: *She'd like me to die.* Then I saw that wild light in her eyes again, and a smile appeared. She leaned forward and whispered: *I'd rather walk the streets!*

Where did *that* come from! It was exciting. For a second I glimpsed her standing in a doorway, in an alley, on a wet night—

—So what happened?

She frowned. She was serious again.

—But Harriet was very lonely, this was before she got sick. She'd come into my bedroom in tears. She'd tell me Daddy was so mean. Then she'd have me stand behind her at the dressing table and brush her hair. She'd watch me in the mirror.

Here she pretended to be her mother and spoke in a languid, singsong voice.

—That's lovely, darling, please don't stop. A little harder. I shouldn't come to you like this but there's nobody else I can talk to. It's all right. He's tired. He doesn't mean it.

Constance looked at me as if to say: You see what he did to her? Outside in the street some madman was cursing Jesus Christ. She then remarked in an offhand manner that of course Harriet was English. So I was right. I understood then that the mother had transmitted something of her Englishness to Constance, and it partly accounted for the attraction she'd aroused in me. Not that I made a fetish of it, being English, I mean, but I did own an English car, a Jaguar. A black Mark VIII four-door sedan with a straight-six engine and twin carburetors. They're quite rare. Barb hated it. She said it was like riding in a hearse.

But Harriet would apparently make Constance stand very straight and inspect her. She'd trace the line of her eyebrow with her finger. Sometimes she told her to undress, then examined her as though she were a specimen of some kind. She never told her why. All this I learned that first night, in these brief bursts of revelation. Meanwhile it took some effort on her part to learn anything about me. But when she found out what I did for a living she was surprised.

—All the smart women at that party and you came after me?

I lifted my hands, palms outspread. I told her I couldn't figure out what she was. That made her laugh.

—You and me both, she said.

★

We found a cab and I let her out in front of a small apartment building on East Fifty-sixth Street near the intersection with First Avenue. I had the cab wait until she was in the door. Then I went on uptown to this big gloomy place of mine on the West Side.

Same thing the next time we met, meaning that after more talk largely concerning her family we parted with some kisses in the back of a cab before I left her, inflamed and abandoned in the lobby of her building, or so she told me later. That wasn't how I remember it—I'd have taken her home with me that first night, if she'd let me—but here was the point, she said she was warming to me and it was a "not unpleasant sensation." I was growing accustomed to her ironic, not to say caustic, not to say occasionally foulmouthed turns of phrase and "a not unpleasant sensation" was I suppose the best I could hope for then. But it did disturb me, the aloofness she communicated at times, the bland detachment, although it never put me off her: the reverse. I wanted to know where it came from. What damage had caused it? How could I make her warm again? She was far more bitter than she had any right to be at her age.

A few days later I took her to the seafood place in Grand Central. It was crowded. At a table littered with empty chowder bowls and clamshells and beer bottles, amid a clamor of voices, and beneath a timbrel-vaulted ceiling of Guastavino tiles, I asked Constance to tell me more about her father. I consider it a mark of an advanced urban civilization when one's private life can be conducted in public.

—Daddy sounds like a depressive, I said. How did your mother deal with that?

She didn't mind my intrusive curiosity now. She willingly offered her experience. She said I made her feel interesting.

—She ignored him. He was always working anyway.

She then told me something she said she hadn't told anybody, not even Iris. She told me she thought Harriet was really a very

47

lonely woman, and that Daddy didn't understand this until she was dying, by which time of course it was too late. Then he was overcome with guilt. He'd been eaten up with guilt ever since. That was why he was such a sour man.

My own thoughts were running on different lines.

—I still don't understand this anger of his, I said.

—What anger?

—At you.

But she hadn't said he was angry at her! I'd inferred it, then asked the question that had obsessed her for years. I saw her sudden alarm. Then she looked down at the table and shook her head.

—I don't know. I wouldn't study medicine but I guess it's more complicated than that.

So I asked her if she resented the loss of her childhood. In fact I said *theft*. She'd had to take on her mother's role when she was barely in her teens and look after Iris.

—Daddy never appreciated me, that's what I resented.

Not even as a small child had she enjoyed anything like the gruff affection Iris apparently got from him. He was crazy about little Iris. He'd lunge for her and lift her high, holding her in his big hands, and shaking her as she shrieked with pleasure. Constance saw a softness in his face then, and a warmth in his cold pale eyes that she'd never known.

—Is that why you hate him?

I was on what Ed Kaplan would call a fishing expedition here. It was unfair of me but she didn't seem to mind.

—I do hate him. Whatever I do, I feel I've failed. He never tries to hide his contempt.

—Contempt! I cried. Isn't he a doctor?

Suddenly she was angry.

—Yes, he's a doctor, so what?

She practically shouted it. Heads turned. She lowered her voice.

—You think doctors don't know about cruelty? You think they're *benign?*

I sat with an elbow on the table, my chin in my palm. I gazed at her. I enjoyed seeing her all stirred up like this. I liked that the impeccably constructed facade could be so easily disordered by a stray remark from out of left field. She thought I was accusing her of exaggerating the whole thing, of saying, in effect, she only hated him because he held her to a higher standard than her sister. She said it was more complicated than that. Sometimes she thought he wanted to kill her and she didn't know why. Feelings like that don't come from nowhere, she said.

She stared at me with fierce intensity. She lifted her chin.

—I've read Freud, she said.

—Oh you have, have you? Shall we get out of here?

There was a third date, and this time she wasn't abandoned, inflamed, in the lobby of her building. She let me take her home. It was a memorable night for many reasons. I think we pleased each other, I know she pleased me. Very late that night, in the darkness, in my bed, she told me she didn't know what love was but it occurred to her that this might be it. She'd never expressed her feelings so plainly before. But me, I *did* know what love was, and I knew that this was it, oh yes, this was it all right, so the next morning I made a bold suggestion. I told her I had to go to London for a few days and did she want to come with me? I said that since

she'd read so many English novels I could use her help as an inter-
preter. It wasn't altogether a joke. She worked in the editorial
department of a publishing company called Cooper Wilder, which
had its offices in one of the old Madison Square skyscrapers. She
needed no persuading.

—Sure, she said.

So we flew Pan Am to the UK. I was doing research for the
book and I needed to look at some papers in the Bodleian. I
planned to stay in the small hotel in Pimlico I always used and
make side trips to Oxford. Constance had been to London once,
in her junior year, but on a tight budget. I won't say I wasn't
anxious about the trip. Despite growing up over there I still
found it difficult at times to penetrate the bland curtain of
conformity behind which my countrymen like to conceal their
true selves.

But I didn't want to sour Constance on the place. She claimed
to love London, or she loved the idea of London, and I feared I'd
have to pretend to be the same, and admire everything as though
I'd just got in from Pittsburgh.

It didn't work out that way. For once it wasn't raining. It was
springtime, there was color in the streets, daffodils in Hyde
Park, love in the air. London seemed a different city from the
one I'd known. This was due to Constance. From the moment
we arrived at our hotel she was sharply alert to the absurdities
of English life. The fact that a grown man in a uniform addressed
her as "madam"—as in, "Would madam care for some tea?"—
this amused her. She said primly that madam would care more
for some gin and tonic. When the man bowed, she bowed

back. I was sitting nearby in the small comfortable lounge. She turned to me and I saw a schoolgirl who'd been mistaken for a lady and had no intention of correcting the error. From then on she conducted herself not as a lady but as an heiress from Texas seriously considering the purchase of anything her delighted eye fell upon. At those times she might seize me by the arm and gasp.

—But Sidney darling, it's too lovely, we must have it at once!

She was peering at an oil painting black with smoke and age that hung over the fireplace in the dining room.

—Honey, I don't think it's for sale.

—Everything's for sale. Daddy told me.

The hotel staff humored her. They behaved with ludicrous formality solely to elicit more of what Constance considered her masterful imitation of a rich American girl. It was hard to say who took greater pleasure in the charade. It helped seal the deal. On our last night, in a restaurant in Piccadilly, after the theater—we'd seen a play by Harold Pinter, an unpleasant, immoral thing, Constance loved it—I made a proposal.

—Do you know what'd be the smart thing for you to do? I said.

She was fond of me that day. She cleared aside the silverware, placed her hands flat on the table, and rested her chin there, gazing up at me.

—What'd be the smart thing for me to do?

I reached over and took her hands in mine.

—The smart thing for you would be to marry me.

She pulled back at once and sat with her arms folded tight across her chest, staring at me, her eyes wide with shock. At times I forgot how young she was. She told me she barely knew me.

—That's not the case. You've just spent five days with me. I don't slap you around, do I? I'm not a lush. I'm a fascinating thinker and I love you. What's not to love back?

She was utterly taken aback. She was deeply embarrassed. She couldn't look at me. It was extraordinary. She'd have laughed if she hadn't known I was serious. But no, she was bewildered. Her father had as good as assured her she'd die a desiccated virgin but apparently not. I didn't tell her I'd brought her to London with this idea already in formation in my mind but I did tell her again that I loved her. But she couldn't even discuss it then and only much later that night did she tell me that five days in a smart London hotel wasn't enough, as a prelude to marriage, and that the idea terrified her, and anyway to make rapid intellectual strides was one thing but this was a direct threat to her autonomy, and anyway she didn't like me. Then she repeated that she barely knew me.

—You know me intimately.

It was true. We'd achieved an impressive degree of intimacy in those few days. I believe I *awakened* her, or aroused her, at least, from a persisting distaste for any kind of sexual contact with a man. But she had such a tricky psyche, all turned in on itself like a convoluted seashell, like a *nautilus*, and at times I caught her *talking to herself* as though in response to what she heard in that seashell. When I asked her who she was talking to she'd all at once startle and wouldn't tell me.

—But what'll happen when we get back to New York?

—Like what?

—I don't know! How can I know until I know you better? You'll get bored with me. I'm not a real intellectual! I'm a cretin. You teach me stuff now, but there's nothing I can teach you.

—That's not true.

I sat up and switched on the bedside lamp. I gazed down at my cretin. She was more lovely at that moment than I ever remembered her, this pale and troubled child. She struggled up and wrapped her arms around her knees.

—What do I teach you? she said, with petulance.

—Yourself.

She stared across the dark room, frowning.

—That's easily mastered, she said.

This was disingenuous. She didn't believe it.

—I don't believe that either, I said quietly.

Tears welled, of course. She nearly surrendered right then and there. But she rallied her resources, I saw it happening. She tried to remember who she thought she was.

—All the same, she said at last, I'm not going to marry you.

★

She held me off for as long as she knew how but in the end she acquiesced. She didn't know what to do and had no friend she trusted well enough to discuss it with other than Ellen Taussig, a senior editor at Cooper Wilder. Ellen was an austere woman of fifty who'd taken Constance under her wing when she'd first arrived in the city two years before. But Ellen had never married and was a fierce believer in the idea that Woman must work,

Woman must rise, Woman must challenge Man. We both knew what she'd say: *Don't do it.*

But I'd arrived at an understanding of Constance by then. For in the long still reaches of the night she'd allowed me a glimpse of her various terrors, childish fears of abandonment mostly, and I had a good idea where they came from. It was the usual tedious story, a failure of approval from the parent. I'd soon put that right, I thought. I'd give her all the approval she wanted.

So it wasn't difficult once she started to waver even a fraction, and I reeled her in with comparative ease. I was patient. I was careful. She came to depend on me. Time spent with me was nourishing, and it was the kind of nourishment she required; this was clear from the first night when we'd sat up talking in that empty restaurant. I offered water, in effect, to a child dying of thirst, although she didn't see it that way at the time. For how do you identify the sickness in yourself, she asked me much later, when we were deep in crisis, and the joking was over, if you've never known a state of health?

I wasn't blind to the responsibility I was assuming. I'd recognized this so-called sickness in her from the start, the impression she gave of an inner fragility, of there being no foundation, or if there was, whether or not it could hold up under pressure. And this was what aroused my love, or my need to protect her, and nourish her, and if this isn't all of love then it's a large part of it, for this was how I'd failed both with Barb and with my first wife, a Frenchwoman I'd met in Oxford when I was a young man and about whom I'd said nothing to Constance. So yes, we decided to get married. She wanted it simple and so did I. We'd do it at City Hall. I think the license cost ten bucks.

We invited only immediate family, which meant my mother, who lived on eastern Long Island, having emigrated with her second husband, an American, soon after my father died, and Constance's father, the doctor, and also her sister, Iris, who both came down from Rhinecliff on the train. Constance said she wished Harriet could have been there, to see her.

★

I was curious to meet the father. Constance hated him, this was abundantly clear. She felt he'd both neglected and punished her and she was obsessed with him. I asked her once about his reaction to his wife's death, this heartless monster, this *doctor*. Did he grieve? He was distraught for months, she said. He'd arrive home late in the evening and sit up drinking. The first she knew of it was one night when she was awakened by a noise and thought a raccoon was in the house. So she went downstairs and tiptoed along the corridor to the kitchen.

She saw him sitting in deep shadow, his long legs stretched out crossed at the ankles and his head on his arms on the table. He was sobbing. That was what she'd heard, her father sobbing. It was pathetic, she said. Not until they were older did she tell her sister about it. Iris was upset by the incident.

—What did you do? she said.

—I went back upstairs.

—You didn't try to comfort him?

—It didn't occur to me.

—Oh, poor Daddy.

They were at another kitchen table when they had this conversation, in New York, and I was present. Something had got them on to Daddy, it never took much. There were times Iris seemed the older of the two, particularly when I saw these sporadic flashes of compassion. I remember she was gazing at Constance with what seemed a kind of compound sympathy both for Daddy's plight, his misery after Harriet's death, and Constance's own, her not knowing how to comfort him. In fact she was never able to. She couldn't reach him, she told me, he was too remote. He rebuffed all attempts she made to get close to him.

She understood this much at least, she said, that he needed to discharge some anger she'd provoked in him. But she hadn't yet learned what she'd done, or what she *was*, what she represented to him, other than a stray girl who happened to live under his roof: a foundling.

—Constance, honey, Iris had said, you're not a foundling. Just trust me, will you? You've had problems with Daddy, god knows we all understand that. So have I. But you're not a foundling.

I was glad she said it: she spared me having to. For some time I'd been aware of a sort of passivity in Constance, a persisting silent claim for sympathy in the face of what she saw as her father's cruelty. It troubled me. I detected no resistance, no defiance, none of the refractory qualities I associate with a healthy spirit. I asked myself if I was unreasonable to think this. I decided I wasn't. The Romantics still have this to teach us, that it's imperative to act and not be acted upon. Constance remained a kind of work in progress. She was unformed and indistinct as yet, and I saw it most clearly when her sister was around. She was still shackled to the conviction that her father had wrecked her life.

THREE

SOON AFTER SHE agreed to marry me I gave Constance a small river view by the nineteenth-century landscape painter Jerome Brook Franklin. It was my first serious gift to her. I wanted her to hang it in her bedroom in New York so she'd see it in the morning when she awoke and be reminded of the view from her bedroom in Ravenswood. It was supposed to arouse happy memories of her childhood. I still believed she must have *some* happy memories.

We were in the sitting room a few nights later, she and I, and the apartment was almost dark. I was lying on the chesterfield, Constance was stretched out on the carpet. She liked to lie on the floor with a cushion under her head. She'd been talking about the painting. Then she was telling me about a flat unmoving expanse of black water that opened off a creek a mile downstream from Ravenswood called Hard Luck Charlie's. This gloomy pond was surrounded by marshland for half a mile, and according to Constance it was haunted by the ghost of an old man who'd had a cabin in the woods nearby. On a hot summer afternoon you could drift for hours in a skiff with only the splash of a fish or the cry of a bird to break the stillness of the place, or a heron wading through the rushes. Daddy had apparently forbidden the girls to take the skiff out on their own but often they disobeyed him. This was around the time Harriet first got sick, she said.

I could all too easily picture it, this pleasant stagnant backwater, the two dreamy girls drifting in a skiff, a drowsy summer afternoon, insects buzzing and the water rank with rotting plant matter. But one day, Constance said, they discovered they'd been observed, and not just observed, reported. It was very bad. Daddy confronted them at breakfast the next morning and asked them if they'd forgotten the rule. Iris had asked him what rule.

—You know what rule, he'd said.

Constance was silent for a few moments. Her mood was somber now. Here it comes, I thought. When they next went down to the boathouse, she said, the skiff wasn't there. Then Iris was kneeling at the end of the dock, gripping the planks and peering down into the water. Constance joined her and she saw what Daddy had done. The skiff was on the bottom of the river. Through the shifting sunlight on the moving water they saw it there, lying on its side in the weeds, rocking slightly in the current. He hadn't told them, he'd let them discover it for themselves. It was an *evil* act, said Constance, so aggrieved you'd have thought it happened yesterday.

—Hardly evil, I said mildly. You'd been told not to take it out.

—For that you scuttle a boat? He took out the bung plug and just let it *sink!*

—He was concerned for your safety.

This made her more angry still.

—No, Sidney, he wasn't, all he wanted was to deprive us of a pleasure. Whose side are you on?

I told her I was always on her side. Then why was I supporting Daddy? I said it's not *supporting*—

—Oh yes it is!

She then told me what it meant. When Daddy scuttled the skiff he was really drowning *her*. Why? Because that's what he'd wanted to do with her ever since she was born, just drown her like an unwanted kitten. Like a needy dependent, she said, some kind of a stray creature who required the shelter of his house but was entitled to none of its warmth, and for damn sure none of its *love*.

—Oh for god's sake, I said.

I found it hard to take her seriously. The story of the scuttled skiff told me more about Constance than it did about him. It was obvious that she didn't understand him. She didn't realize he was only concerned for her welfare. Any father would do the same.

—Sweetheart, I said, he didn't want to drown you.

She sat up and stared at me.

—Oh yes he fucking did, she said.

When she started to swear at me there was no point continuing the conversation. It was very discouraging. And an earlier conversation hadn't helped, when she'd told me I was too old for her. I couldn't seem just to shrug it off. I found it all too easy to imagine her meeting a younger man and, yes, being tempted to stray. This was probably foolish thinking on my part but entirely predictable. It's an ancient simian anxiety, no man is exempt. I'd become not *suspicious,* exactly, but alert. In those days I liked to bring my graduate students home and the apartment would often be full of vigorous young men conducting boisterous arguments about Byron or Goethe or the divine afflatus of Samuel Taylor Coleridge. Here life was noisily lived, and although Constance was usually too tired to take part in my informal seminars, when she did join us I'd take notice of which of my students she responded to more warmly than was strictly necessary.

This would provoke another argument. Once again I was accused of various crimes of the heart and had to defend myself. There were tears and screams and even the breaking of glassware and crockery. It was exhausting but it ended, as before, in bed, where all was forgiven and a tentative peace accord established. I soon abandoned the informal seminars. So yes, she kept me vigilant. She also kept me at a pitch of anxious exhilaration that I hadn't known since the early days with Barb. Ed Kaplan saw the difference in me. He told me I looked ten years younger.

—I was right about you, he said.

—What do you mean by that?

—You need a wife.

We were crossing an uptown campus, I remember, on our way to lunch. I asked him to explain himself.

—Sidney, where else besides marriage can you find yourself in a moral predicament on a daily basis? You're one of those men who's got to be forever choosing to do the right thing so as to silence the voices in your head.

—What voices?

—Guilty voices.

—What am I supposed to be so guilty about?

—Your controlling personality. Your inability to tolerate criticism—

—Okay, Ed, that's enough.

He'd missed the point. As for voices in the head, that wasn't my problem. We walked on in silence. We crossed Broadway. We were too slow with the light and a taxi driver screamed insults at us out the window of his cab. The death of urban civility was one of my preoccupations at the time. I saw it as another symptom of the city's deepening malaise.

—Ed, that may all be true but it doesn't change the fact that sometimes I feel like I'm dealing with a—

I couldn't finish the sentence. I was going to say *paranoid hysteric*.

—Relax. It's good for you.

But at times I was starting to wonder if I hadn't made a mistake, and once or twice I even thought of the quiet years with Barb with nostalgia. And regarding Barb, there was a new development, not a happy one, and it did nothing to improve my state of mind. The last time I'd seen her she'd told me there was something wrong with her. She had to go into the hospital for a few tests.

We'd been sitting in the kitchen of her small rented house in Atlantic City, not far from the beach. I was alarmed. She was lethargic. There was puffiness around her eyes. Her skin was sickly looking. She'd lost weight. Wearily she pushed a hand through her hair.

—What about Howard?

—He'll go to my mother's.

I thought of Queenie Mulcahy with her cigarettes and her gin, and her phlegmy cough, and her endless stories about her life as a showgirl—

—He could stay with us, I said.

—What about Constance?

Barb summoned for this question a spark of friendly malice.

—She'd like to get to know him, I said.

—That's not what I heard.

She gazed at me with lifted eyebrows and the ghost of a smile. For a second she was her old self. How do women know these things about one another? I told her it was time Constance and Howard met. Barb shouldn't worry. It would all be fine.

—Your funeral, she said.

She wasn't the type to try to protect her boy from life's complications. She knew, too, what sort of a boy he was, nothing if not self-sufficient. So I called him in from the yard.

★

We were to meet Iris and the doctor off the train at Penn Station. Tarpaulins hung like great dirty curtains obscuring the high spaces of the roof from view. We picked our way through heaps of planks and scaffolding. There was dust in the air and the place was raucous with shouting men and jackhammers. Constance was tense. She could barely speak to me. Her anxiety about the wedding was aggravated by the prospect of her father's arrival. She'd spent the previous night in my apartment. She'd paced the floor, twisting her hands together as I sat reading. I understood how difficult this was for her. She was a high-strung immature young woman about to take a large step into the unknown with a man she'd known for less than a year. Also, her father, that stern and bitter man, whom she felt she'd always disappointed, would be watching her. She stopped pacing and stared at me.

—Aren't you frantic? she cried.

I had her sit on my lap and I put my arms around her. She clung to me like a child.

—No.

—But why not?

How was I to tell her that my impulse to protect and nourish her was as vital for my own welfare as it was for hers? I didn't think she could understand this yet. My love was grounded as much in moral conviction as it was in affection and desire, but she didn't know me very well. She didn't know what she had in me. She was very young. I asked her to trust me.

—I don't think I can, she whispered.

It was starting to get dark outside but we didn't turn the lamps on. I put my book down. She sat on the floor beside the chesterfield, and as the shadows gathered around us she reached up and slipped her hand in mine. We sat in silence. She gripped my hand tight. She grew calm at last. I wanted her to feel that she'd never be exposed to danger again, not as long as I was there. I couldn't explain what I was afraid of, but I feared for her, and that was why I was marrying her. If I didn't do this I felt I had no business being around her. I didn't know what more I could offer her.

I saw the doctor before she did. Two figures emerged from the rear of the train and paused for a few seconds on the platform, engaged in what looked like a quarrel. The girl was about twenty, the man much older. It could only be them. Then they were advancing upon us, and when the girl saw Constance—she was Iris, of course—she dropped her suitcase and ran toward us with her arms spread wide, shouting. Constance, laughing and blushing, was crushed to the body of her sister, and it was for me to step forward and greet the father.

—Doctor Schuyler. Sidney Klein, I said.

He was a tall man, as tall as I, and he looked me up and down as we gravely shook hands. I was impressed with his gravitas. A man of the old school, I thought, salt of the American earth. It takes a couple of centuries to make one of these. What did he make of me? I had money, yes, and I had tenure, but I was an Englishman and he wouldn't know if I was to be trusted. High above us pigeons fluttered in the iron trelliswork and the locomotive released a prolonged hiss. On the platform the last of the passengers streamed around us, leaving the sisters clinging together, and myself with the father. Stranded between us was the suitcase Iris had abandoned in the middle of the platform.

—You'd better call me Morgan, he said.

—Sidney, I said.

That night we dined together in a steakhouse on Lexington Avenue. It was a noisy, steamy place, all bustle and meaty smells: I thought the doctor would like it. I was aware of the momentous nature of the occasion and I think he was too. He was a reserved man in his late sixties, spare, deliberate, and quietly amusing, particularly in response to the more extravagant claims of Iris, who was excited to be in New York and in particular in this large room full of loud talk and quick-witted waiters with whom she bantered happily. She was a college senior, majoring in biology at a school upstate, but unmistakably the same grinning, gap-toothed girl I'd seen in Constance's photograph. I kept an eye on the sisters but I reserved my close attention for the father. Constance wanted me to believe that his antagonism toward her had made her the unhappy woman she was, but having now met the man I didn't buy it. He was gruff, but he was a man of the old school. They're supposed to be gruff. But he was also tender, and he was watchful. When Iris let out a shriek that had other diners turning in our direction, he laid a finger briefly on her wrist and she grew quiet at once. When the waiter approached to refill her glass, not for the first time, Dr. Schuyler caught the man's eye and silently voiced the word *no*. I saw this, and he saw me seeing it, and we exchanged not so much a smile as a mutual glance of amused understanding.

—Daddy, will you please tell Constance that a virus is a germ?

—Constance, your sister believes that a virus is a germ.

—Yes, but what sort of a germ? She doesn't know!

—Of course I know!

Then, in a low voice, pleading: Daddy, I'd like another glass of wine.

—I know you would, but you won't get it.

I watched Constance at times react to Iris like a mother, with impatient shakes of the head and a lifting of her eyes to the ceiling. At other times she was drawn into the girl's restless stream of talk. When Iris amused her she'd lean forward with her jaw falling in disbelief.

—Iris, *you can't say that!*

—I just did.

Daddy might or might not adjudicate the matter. Halfway through the meal I realized I was no closer to answering the question that concerned me: how Constance got to be so helpless and at times so very *numb*. I no longer believed her father was a cruel man, or that he'd done her irreparable harm. I'd seen nothing to support that idea. It occurred to me that Iris might in her carelessness have done her a more subtle injury although I couldn't imagine what it might be. Constance told me once that her sister wanted her to die, but every younger sibling feels that way. She said her father wanted her dead too. It occurred to me that one day she'd think the same of me.

While I watched them, they watched me. The doctor's manner toward me was affable but undemonstrative. I'd passed some kind of a test—I wasn't an out-and-out cad—and he was in no hurry to force the acquaintance. Time would serve us in that regard. I was of course much older than Constance, and this counted in my favor. As for Iris, she was eager to see some display of prowess from the man about to marry her sister.

—So Sidney, how smart are you, scale of one to ten?

Elbows planted on the table, leaning in, gazing at me with bright-eyed, vinous warmth, clearly she'd been told by Constance that I was a brainy chap.

—Twelve.

—You have to say that but I'm serious. How would you fix the problems of New York?

—No, Iris, don't do this to him, said Constance.

—How long have I got? I said.

—Iris is eager to be mugged, said the doctor. We could put her down in an alley on the way back to the hotel.

—I'm not afraid of New York, she cried. When I live here I'll never be mugged!

This bravura statement provoked various reactions all at once. I asked her how she'd achieve invulnerability where so many before her had tried and failed. For it was becoming apparent that nobody was safe here anymore.

—Sidney, she said, laying a hand on my arm, trust me.

When the meal ended and we rose to our feet, that section of the tablecloth controlled by Iris resembled the sort of blighted neighborhood she was confident she could survive in. It was a mess of salt, crusts of bread, ash, spilled coffee, burned-out tenement buildings and broken government. She moved at once to her father's side and slipped her arm in his.

—I'll take this old man home, she said. Constance can have the other one.

—You're such a child, said Constance.

When I kissed Iris good night, she murmured in my ear.

—Sidney, with Constance it's important to wind her up regularly, otherwise she runs down.

As I hailed a cab I thought it a not unperceptive remark. But a woman isn't a clock! A clock can't decide what time it is, its movements are determined by its mechanism. And I asked myself, not for the first time, if the same could be said of Constance, and was that what Iris meant?

We were all subdued in the morning when we met outside City Hall. It was a clear, cool day. City Hall is a fine old public building in the classical manner. It has a white portico with pillars. Inside, there's a rotunda with a grand marble staircase. Abraham Lincoln

lay in state there. As did Ulysses S. Grant. In the park over which
City Hall presides stands the statue of one of my heroes, Nathan
Hale. He was hanged by the British early in the War of Independence. On the gallows he said he regretted having but one life to
give for his country. He was a foolish boy but he certainly showed
courage at the end, but when I told Constance the story she
yawned. She said she'd heard it already.

We were shown into a large waiting room to join the other
prospective brides and grooms and their families. It was as richly
diverse a cross section of the city's grand mosaic as you could hope
to see. We sat on hard benches until we were called in to go before
the judge. Constance clung to me, and not for the first time I felt
a whisper of anxiety. She was a mystery to me, this pale serious
girl, she was opaque, oblique—what was I thinking of? Iris was
watching me. She knew what I was thinking of. Grinning that
toothy grin of hers, she made a small private solidarity gesture with
her fist, and from that moment I loved her like a brother.

When it was all over we walked to the old Italian restaurant on
Chambers Street. My mother had arrived from Long Island earlier
that morning. She was dressed all in black for reasons nobody
understood. She'd acquired many eccentricities over the course of
her long widowhood. It was oddly wonderful to see the doctor, in
his dark suit, himself a reserved and formal man, loom over my
equally reserved and formal mother and bend to shake her tiny
hand. At the restaurant Iris succeeded in doing what she'd been
prevented from doing the previous night, she made a fool of
herself, not being accustomed to champagne. I had to take her
outside and help her throw up in a parking lot.

Later that evening Constance was depressed. She said Daddy had once told her she shouldn't have any illusions about New York. He said she'd last a few months in the city, a year at most, and then come home to Ravenswood and look after him. But she'd made her way in publishing and found a husband. She was now Mrs. Klein. But she couldn't help comparing herself to the other Mrs. Klein, the diminutive black-veiled widow, my mother. She said she felt like a variation on a theme: my mother at an early stage of development, like a chrysalis, a little black widow in the making.

—For god's sake, I said, it's our wedding night.

—I'm sorry. It's how I feel.

FOUR

CONSTANCE WAS UNFAMILIAR with the old prewar apartments of the Upper West Side. Mine, though dark, was large. After we were married I watched her drift through my rooms, nervous and hesitant, glancing into shadowy corners as though they concealed malevolent intruders. She told me she was easily spooked. She also felt that at any moment she'd be unmasked as a trespasser and evicted. She said that after her mother died she hadn't felt at home in her father's house either. I did what I could to make her feel welcome. I told her that the apartment was her home now. I wanted her to get used to her new surroundings in her own time, as you would a cat. Eventually I realized that her reluctance to settle masked a persisting unease not with the apartment but with me. Of course the only man she'd lived with before me was her father. One day she told me she was still mystified as to why I'd chosen her. I remember I gazed at her fondly. I told her she'd looked so helpless at that book party I knew I had to do something about it.

—Do you know how many predators there are in this town? I said.

She was faintly displeased.

—You make me feel like a gazelle.

—You *are* a gazelle.

There was more than a grain of truth in this, and when I'd convinced her I was joking it briefly became a game we played in the bedroom. She was the graceful leaping antelope, I was the greedy lion. She couldn't escape me, and our tussles were vigorous. Then one night, as we lay panting in tangled bed sheets, she sat up and told me that because I was the one she woke up with in the morning, and the one she went to bed with at night, it was true, she couldn't escape me, *ever*.

—Not ever, Sidney! she cried.

Then she delivered the bad news.

—I don't think it's working.

—What isn't working?

—The marriage.

I stayed calm. I'd anticipated this. It was taking longer than it should have to get her established in my home but I believed it would all come good given enough *time*.

—Sweetheart, why not?

—I think I've made a mistake.

I asked her quietly what the mistake was. We'd moved to the kitchen for this conversation. She'd made herself a pot of tea. Her answer was unsatisfactory. She spoke slowly, as though reciting a lesson learned in class. I remembered her once claiming to have read Freud. Now she told me she understood why she'd agreed to marry me. Her father never gave her what she needed, she said, and she'd always felt it was her fault.

I understood the argument. She'd lost her mother at a time when a girl most needs a mother, and was then given charge of her younger sister. Daddy hadn't been supportive. He was more often absent than present. He'd actively discouraged her from moving to New York. When he saw that he couldn't stop her he told her she wouldn't succeed. He was overly critical and he made her feel worthless. But unlike most of the population of New York City she wouldn't see a psychiatrist. She said she already knew what was wrong with her. So how was she going to get better? She'd get better, she said, when Daddy wasn't in the picture anymore.

—You're waiting for your father to *die?*

—He can't go on forever.

Constance and I have been over this material in depth and in detail. At the time I said to her that her anger toward her father was childish. It was too easy to blame the father. Everyone blamed the father. It was lazy liberal thinking, I told her. I didn't see him as a monster, I said. He and I got along fine. I liked the man.

But Constance was indifferent to my opinion. Instead she said that from the moment she'd met me she'd wanted *me* for her father, so that she could start over. So that she could *make good*, by which she meant repair whatever it was she'd got wrong with Daddy. She said it was a *repetition compulsion complex*.

She peered at me anxiously. My first reaction was one of amused disbelief, but I showed her nothing of this. Instead I nodded as though I took the idea seriously.

—A *repetition compulsion complex?*

But she was never at her best in theoretical discussion. She didn't have that kind of a mind. What kind of a mind she *did* have, this I hadn't yet discovered.

—Yes.

—And it means the marriage won't work?

—Please don't look at me like that. *I can't be your wife! I can't be anyone's wife!*

—Why not?

—I don't know!

—You want me to explain it to you?

She regarded me with suspicion. I remembered Iris's remark: It's important to wind her up regularly, otherwise she runs down. She was run-down now. She had to be run-down to tell me I was her father. She sat there in her bathrobe, her hair tousled, her skin very clear, her lips moving just a little as though in silent colloquy with some unseen being. She was bewildered by the turn the conversation had taken. I was warm, gentle, solicitous.

—Constance, honey, I'm not your father.

—I know that—

—*I'm not your father.* I'm your husband. Your father abandoned you emotionally because he was grieving. It's not so unusual. But I'm not him. I've made a commitment to you and I won't let you down.

—You let Barb down.

—All the more reason.

—You let Howard down.

Fortunately she knew nothing about my first wife, about whom the less said the better. But as long as she wanted to hurt me I felt

I had something to work with. It was indifference I dreaded, and I knew she was capable of it.

—Why won't you let me introduce you to Howard? I said.

—He already has a mother. Don't change the subject. You treat me like I'm one of your students. Have you got any cigarettes?

By this time she was pacing the floor. It was early October and still warm outside. The window was open and the mayhem on the street was getting started, a few random screams, a burst of manic laughter. There was a pack of cigarettes on top of the refrigerator, Ed Kaplan had left them. I gave her one and threw the rest in the trash.

—I try not to treat you like a student but if I do it's only because I want to teach you what I know. There was a time you liked that.

—I've been educated already.

I may have made a brief display of the mildest skepticism, some tiny reflex of an eyebrow, perhaps. But she saw it. She stopped pacing and glared at me. Her eyes filled with tears. I was on my feet at once, then she was trembling in my arms. Then she pushed me away.

—I won't back down! she screamed. You like students who argue with you and then back down but I won't!

There was more of this. She was angry, first, that I was an unsatisfactory father, and second, that I was an overbearing professor. She told me I had no interest in who she was, only in how she conformed to the image of her I'd constructed in my mind. Only in what I could make her *into*.

—You're too old for me! You were *selfish* to make me marry you and I can't believe I was such a fool!

I turned away. I lifted my arms, I shrugged my shoulders. Later there were tearful apologies and she clung to me in bed, appalled at what she'd said. I relented. I comforted her. I told her that her urge to cause me pain was really an expression of love. I said she wouldn't go to all the trouble if she didn't care about me. She seized gratefully on this idea. Then there was more sex and it was always better after that. No postcoital *tristesse* in my bedroom.

★

And so the fall passed, and then we were driving up to Ravenswood for Christmas and Howard was with us, poor kid, and missing his mother, for Barb was again in the hospital. The day was cold and clear but traffic was heavy and the journey was slow. By the time we got to the house he was tired. He'd been in the car too long. Constance said she hoped we'd be given a drink on arrival but Daddy didn't like her to ask before it was offered. Once he'd withheld it until dinner so as to punish her. It never happened with Iris, she said. Hearing this I knew why I was dreading the next days. It wouldn't be much of a Christmas for Howard, with Constance in such a foul state of mind, and so very antagonistic toward her father.

There he stood on the porch between those peeling Corinthian pillars, a tall, sparely built figure in a thick black cardigan and baggy corduroy trousers. He could have been an American poet, one of the mad grand old men just beginning his decline. The light spilled out from the open front door behind him and was reflected off the snow. The tower on the southwest corner stood out sharp against the dusk, and beyond the house the pines were a mass of blackness.

Constance had once told me her heart always quickened at the sight of the river far below and the mountains beyond, where the last of the day made a thin band of red in the sky, but she seemed indifferent to it now.

The old man bent down to greet Howard as he climbed the steps of the porch. He took the boy's hand, then turned back into the house. The stoop in his posture had worsened since we'd last seen him over the Labor Day weekend. I felt a sudden tenderness for him. It was clear that his strength was ebbing, and that soon he'd be frail.

I got out of the car and unloaded the suitcases from the trunk. Constance wore an expression of such sour and weary resignation that I told her to please make an effort, for her father's sake if not for mine. Together we walked across the icy driveway and up the steps of the porch.

Two days later came the doctor's shattering revelation, and that's when everything properly went to hell.

FIVE

ALL THAT FALL my sister Iris put on a brave face in public but when she was by herself she drank. I was the only one she talked to about Eddie Castrol but I soon grew impatient with her and then she didn't confide in me anymore. What a relief that was. Sidney and I had a quiet period. He was busy with his book. I think he was having a good deal of trouble with it. With writers it's best to leave them alone at times like this. They only snap at you if you try to help. No one can help me now, he'd say, like a drowning man. My only real pleasure in life was his boy, Howard. He was with us for Thanksgiving and again for the Christmas holiday. We were going up to Ravenswood. I wasn't looking forward to it.

Oh, Ravenswood. That goddamn house. How I hated it. To me it was hell. I hadn't known a day of happiness in that house since Harriet died. I'd once believed that when at last I left I would never return. Ha. It pulled me back. It sucked me in. We turned off the river road and into the drive. It was late afternoon and the fog was rolling up from the river. The pines were shrouded but not the tower. It had a peaked cone on top and a spire with a weathervane. It was an absurd piece of folly, built by Daddy's grandfather. It even had stained-glass windows. At the front of the house there was a long porch supported by a row of columns badly in need of a coat of paint, as was everything else. And not just paint: Roof shingles fell off every winter and the top floor was in a perpetual state of dripping damp. There was also a screened verandah in poor repair with rotting wicker tables and chairs dangerous to sit in. As Sidney parked by the barn a few crows lifted from the rooftop and disappeared noisily into the fog. Cue the monster. Daddy appeared.

Inside the house it was no better. There was a long dark hall with a hardwood floor and two huge hideous Victorian chests of drawers pushed against the walls with rubbish heaped on top, old books, unopened mail, keys to doors to rooms nobody ever entered anymore. Portraits of the forgotten dead hung from thin wires attached to the molding. There were large patches of damp on the ceiling. The drawing room was off to the left with windows facing south toward the river. Halfway down the hall was the front staircase, a curving thing of dark heavy wood. Everywhere you looked there was dark heavy wood, and it sure as hell darkened our spirits too. Beyond the staircase stood a grandfather clock, defunct, of course, and a door giving on to a narrow corridor with a lavatory under the back stairs, and the kitchen beyond, and then the back parts of the house. Oh, rally, my sinking heart, for Christ's sake, I thought. It's fucking Christmas.

As a child I tried to have as little as possible to do with the front of the house, and Iris was the same. We used the back stairs, and if we had to be indoors we made ourselves at home in the servants' rooms and the tower, which was unoccupied, until Mildred Knapp moved in and took it over for herself. There was a rounded archway that connected the front and back stairs on the second floor and we treated it as a border crossing. The front of the house was a foreign country with all its hideous furniture and rotting drapes, its big Chinese vases and marble busts of great men that I taught Iris to spit at when nobody was looking. Daddy got in a great temper one time when he found fresh spit all over Franklin Roosevelt. No, the back part of the house was our sovereign nation, a small but plucky republic, population two girls plus dogs. Also a collection of stuffed birds, crows mostly, or birds of the crow kind, corvines. There was even a raven. We assembled them in what we called the Crow Room. It was where we held meetings, Iris and I. From the window we could watch real crows drinking rainwater that had collected in old mossy urns and troughs in the garden below. The sounds of the household were muffled up there. All we'd hear was the faint chiming of some old clock, the distant barking of a dog. Daddy shouting. We also had great sweeping panoramic vistas of the river. Nobody used those rooms except Iris and me.

I spent much of my childhood gazing out of the windows up there. The garden at the back of the house was sad. It was untended because Daddy couldn't afford any ground staff, or so he claimed. Poison ivy clung to everything. It twined its leaves like funeral wreaths around old statues of nymphs and satyrs. There were creeping vines too, and old bits of rusting iron fence.

But the romance of it was the stand of tall dark pine trees that gave the house its name, although I think I never actually saw a raven, only crows. Then below the wood was a swampy stretch beside the railroad tracks and the river. And of course the blue Catskills on the other side. I was vague with Sidney about how long we'd had the place. In fact it had been in the family since 1861, when it was just a modest villa. It was Daddy's grandfather who turned it into a gothic horror house. This was old Augustus Schuyler. *Eccentric* was an understatement, applied to him.

That first night of the holiday we ate in the kitchen, a long, low-ceilinged room with glass-fronted wooden cabinets containing crockery and glassware. There was an ancient wood-burning stove against the back wall. This was Mildred Knapp's domain. I talked to her that first night before she went off to the tower. She told me what I already knew, that the old man didn't have enough to occupy himself. He was bored and often depressed. She said that if it wasn't for her he wouldn't see anybody. So nobody visits him anymore, I said.

—There's not so many of us left who knew him in the old days, said Mildred.

I went back into the kitchen. It was the only warm room in the house. The boiler had never been replaced. It was loud and unreliable and now there was a problem with the radiators. A man from the village had told Daddy they had to be drained but that he couldn't do it until after the holiday. So we were dependent for warmth on electric heaters and log fires. More than anything in the world I hate being cold. I felt it more acutely than the rest of them. I was wearing my winter coat indoors, and my scarf and gloves. Daddy displayed a grim satisfaction in our predicament. He'd been having trouble with the heating all winter, he said. I told him he should have come down to the city.

—Better here, he said.

He imagined it would be some sort of adventure, to live in a cold house in midwinter. Blazing fires and thick sweaters, a scene from his youth, I guess.

—It's intolerable. I'm frozen. We all are.

—Frozen?

—Yes, Daddy, *frozen.*

The reality of three adults and a small boy in discomfort rudely awakened him. His tone became brusque. It was an old man's folly and his irritation with himself was painful to observe. I told Sidney that after Harriet died I'd found it hard at first to spend time in the kitchen. If there was a room in the house where her ghost resided, that was it. He asked me if I believed in ghosts and I told him I did. I said the Hudson Valley was infested with them, positively swarming with them. But how long can you avoid a kitchen? That night Howard was happy enough in the big armchair by the woodstove. He never complained. He could amuse himself for hours with a piece of string or better still a mousetrap. He'd found one in his bedroom and brought it downstairs. A little later I heard a small gasp. He'd sprung the trap on his thumbnail. But he made no further noise. Carefully he released his thumb, then put it in his mouth and sucked it.

—Howard, I whispered, did that hurt?

He looked up at me, and still sucking his thumb he nodded his head several times. The nail would turn black in a day or two. What a brave boy. Then Daddy wanted to know how Iris was.

—I've seen her better, I said.

—It'll be easier for her soon.

—How?

I wasn't paying attention. I was still gazing at Howard.

—When she's finished her hospital training. Then you remember what it's like to sleep again.

He didn't realize that Iris wouldn't be starting medical school until next fall—if then. If ever! Sidney turned to me, frowning. He didn't like these mistakes Daddy was making. First the radiators, now Iris.

—She'll tell you when she gets here, I said.

He was sitting forward in an old wing chair by the woodstove. He was staring at the floor, his elbows on his knees and his hands hanging loose between them. Even at seventy he was a graceful man, cold and mean and graceful, like one of Sidney's dead poets. *He walks in beauty, like the night.* Ha. It was the long arms and legs, the long fingers and the spareness of his frame. He'd always had that grace. Sidney said it lent him authority and he'd needed it, doctoring in the Hudson Valley.

—You two love each other?

He was still staring at the kitchen floor, and for a second I thought he meant Sidney and me. But he was talking about Iris. Of course we did, I said.

—There's something I have to tell you.

—Sure.

—Tomorrow then.

As we lay awake that night in a cold bed I asked Sidney what he thought Daddy wanted to tell me. He said it was his will. He didn't want his daughters to have a falling-out over his will. That was why he needed to know we loved each other. I asked him to turn over. Then I pressed myself against his back. I wanted all the warmth he could give me.

The day dawned clear and cold and it wasn't easy to get out of bed. Mine was a large bedroom with a fireplace with a mantel and various paintings on the wall chosen by me for their ugliness. There was a large selection of ugly paintings in the attic. Old carpets were laid overlapping on the floorboards and the bed had been around for at least a hundred years. But the room had a western exposure so you could see the Hudson when you woke up, if you left a gap between the drapes. We could hear Howard in the corridor outside our room. I pulled on my bathrobe and stood at the window. Sidney said he was starting to appreciate the Hudson Valley: There was sublimity here, he said. The mood of the river had changed. Yesterday there'd been a kind of calm drift, today it was tossing up white crests where the wind whipped across it. I asked him what the word *sublimity* meant.

—The effect of novelty on ignorance. That's Dr. Johnson.

—But what do you think?

—It's a word we use to represent the unrepresentable.

Not bad. Suddenly the bedroom door was flung open. There was Howard, in a rare state of excitement, clapping his hands and shouting about the *cold!*

—Come here! I cried. Into bed with me!

Later, in the kitchen, I expected Daddy to suggest we have our talk but he said nothing about it so I said nothing either. I think he hadn't slept well. He'd told me once that having slept well all his life he was finding it difficult. We'd been sitting at the kitchen table first thing in the morning, this was in September, Labor Day. I was attempting to be friendly. He'd wake at four, he said, and be unable to get back. But he wouldn't take anything that might help him sleep. I asked him whether he'd prescribed sleeping pills for his patients.

—Certainly I did but I won't use them myself.

—Why not?

He was slow in speech and he liked to be precise. He found it difficult to look at me when we talked of anything at all personal. As in this conversation.

—I don't want to have to depend on the things.

—Does it matter?

Up came his head then, and as the early sun caught his face I had the full blaze of those cold pale eyes of his.

—Constance, this may surprise you but I prefer not to be addicted to any substance.

—What do you think about at four in the morning?

—I think foolish thoughts. I think about futility and I become fearful. I feel afraid.

—Of death?

—Yes, of death.

I never know what the best next step is when a conversation reaches this point.

—I guess that's what God's for, I said. Isn't that what God's for, Daddy, to give us the illusion of something still to come?

Widowed and alone, godless, somber in temperament and determined to see through his harsh dreadful nights without sleeping pills, he brushed this idea aside. When I asked him the next morning how he'd slept he made a brief evasive response the meaning of which was clear: off-limits. Mind your own business. He regretted speaking to me about it and it wouldn't happen again.

Later I mentioned the conversation to Iris.

—Oh, he's terrified of dying, she said.

—But he's seen so much of it.

—It doesn't help. It starts to wear off when it gets light outside.

I could imagine it. Sleepless at dead of night the mind is vulnerable to a host of demons, and only much later did I discover what his looked like. But now he wanted to talk to me, and because he seemed unable to broach the topic Sidney thought it must be about his will. Sidney said that to a man who fears death a conversation about your last will and testament is not a joyous prospect.

He chose his moment on Christmas afternoon. We'd had our big meal in the middle of the day. Sidney had taken Howard for a walk in the woods. He wanted him tired out so he'd go to bed early and sleep through the night. Daddy had built a fire in the drawing room. I hated that room most of all. Dusty Victorian furniture and tall windows that no longer fitted their frames. Ancient velvet drapes to keep out the wind, a grand piano at the far end that nobody ever played. Carpets that still smelled of dog and urine. He'd been feeding the fire for hours. It crackled and spat, it flung embers over the fireguard that left scorch marks on the rug. He sat close to the hearth in his armchair. I was lying on the couch with a blanket spread over my legs. We each had a book. Everything was quiet. The light was fading from the sky and then I heard the beginnings of a whisper as the windows shivered and the wind came gusting down the chimney. I couldn't concentrate on what I was reading. He wasn't reading either. He asked me when Iris was coming.

He'd been told this already but I said she'd be on the early train and I'd go in and pick her up from the station. Familiar information is a comfort to the old.

—Constance, I have to tell you something, he then said.

—Sure, Daddy.

A silence. Then he told me.

—I'm not your father.

I had to ask him to repeat it. I picked up the poker from the hearth and thrust it into the fire. Flames went surging up the chimney as the logs shifted. I saw cathedrals in there, penitentiaries, infernos. I was in shock. A world had started to collapse but I didn't know that because it hadn't gathered momentum yet.

—Constance, leave the fire alone.

—It's getting cold in here.

I didn't intend a reference to anything other than the temperature of the room. I was still in my overcoat. I thought: Sidney will be back with Howard soon, and the boy will be chilled. He should be taken home tonight. We should all go home tonight. But why had it taken him so long to tell me? And thinking this, I realized it confirmed a message I'd been hearing all my life, and a kind of dam burst inside me. I cried out, but why now? *Why now?*—and he said he felt I should know the truth before it was too late.

—Too *late?* I whispered in disbelief.

What of course he meant was too late for *him*, because he wanted to die unburdened of his secret. I told him I should have been told as soon as I was old enough to make sense of it. What was I supposed to do with it now? If I wasn't his daughter then who was I?

—Is my father alive?

—No.

I didn't absorb this immediately. I was on my feet now, standing over him, pushing my fingers through my hair.

—So who was he?

—A man your mother knew.

—Oh, a *man*, I said, turning away, and Harriet knew him. What a relief that is. So who am I, Daddy?

He wouldn't tell me. All he said was, it was important that I know the truth. I disagreed. Pacing back and forth between the window and the fireplace, and weeping now, I said I didn't understand why I had to be told at all. What good could it do me now, the truth? Oh, the *truth*—! I spat the word out. I said sometimes the truth is no better than a *whip*—

—How can I make you understand?

I sat down. I was trying not to cry. How did he imagine he could ever make me understand? In my mind's eye I'd seen a drawer torn violently from a desk and turned upside down so its contents spilled out. Letters, photographs, invoices, checks, objects charged with meaning and others of no significance whatever, all scattered on the floor in disorder. The prospect then of gathering them up and attempting to sort them out. In all the cacophony I was unable to isolate any single thought. Memories arose, each one demanding to be reorganized or reconstructed in light of this new information. Why had he told me *now?* Then: I'd always known it. He'd always withheld a father's love and for this simple reason, that he wasn't my father. Then I understood why he'd been such a vindictive man, it was obvious, it was because I was the living embodiment of my mother's infidelity, of her *sin*. I reminded him of Harriet's sin and, too, of his failure, for no woman ever cheated on a man without it being his own fault.

He was Iris's father and he wasn't mine and he'd told me so a thousand times—

A question occurred to me. Later I wished I'd never asked it.

—Does Iris know?

—Yes.

I left the room and closed the door. What he'd said had undermined my whole idea of who I was, not a sturdy construction to begin with. Now he'd told me that Iris knew, *and she'd never said a word*. I stood in the cold corridor with my back to the door. His words kept sweeping through my mind, over and over. Dimly I supposed I should ask him again who my real father was but I could imagine the tawdry narrative he'd produce, Harriet's secret, her exposure, his anger, her shame, her eventual capitulation to his insistence that I never be told. Her early death, doubtless hastened by his corrosive rage. All this flooding through me as I stood with my back to the door, my heart racing and my breath coming in shallow gulps. I wanted a cigarette, where could I get one now? I was about to go upstairs when the front door opened and a still colder air entered the house.

Sidney told me later that he realized as soon as he walked through the front door that Daddy had upset me. I went to him. He took me in his arms.

—I want to go back to the city now, tonight, I whispered.

—What's happened?

I think I was close to hysteria. All I wanted was to leave that cold house and return to New York. I didn't want any details or any background. I just wanted to forget that the conversation had ever occurred.

—Constance, tell me what happened.

—It's too cold here.

—Let's go in to the fire, he said.

He was concerned for Howard, who was peering up at me, his little face parched with cold.

—You go in, I said, I'll be in later. Close the door behind you. Don't let the heat out.

He didn't want to leave me but Howard's teeth were chattering. I went down the hall to the kitchen and left the house by the back door. My breath was like smoke in the night air. A mist was rising from the river. There was frost on the snow already, it crunched beneath my boots as I ran across the grass behind the house and through the trees, then made a rapid, reckless descent, slipping and stumbling down the slope to the marshy stretch by the railroad tracks where ice had formed in the puddles between the clumps of sedge. It splintered under my boots and then I was running across the railroad tracks. I paused, panting, at the edge of the river. It was crowded with jagged chunks of ice.

I stepped onto the dock with caution. Some of the planks were firm, others were splintered and rotten. The pilings were unsteady. Gingerly I walked to the end. I was calmed by the mist all around me. A few yards out a low escarpment of shale broke the surface of the water, a clump of skinny sycamores sprouting from cracks in the rock. I felt an impulse to give myself to the river but I was put off by all the ice. I could imagine drowning, but what I couldn't face was going down in that icy water and freezing to death.

I stared at the old boathouse, derelict now, and that night it seemed more sinister than it had before. I turned away and as I did so those awful words from my mother's funeral came back to me: *He didn't know what hit him.*

When I got back up to the house I went straight into the sitting room. The two men fell silent at once. The air stank of bad faith. Sidney had already taken Howard up to bed.

—Would anybody like a drink? I said in what I hoped were neutral tones. I wished not to give the impression of being hysterical or in any way out of control. Daddy, is there any drink left in the house?

There was a bottle of rum in the kitchen cupboard. Sidney rose to fetch it but I insisted he stay with Daddy. I sat at the kitchen table by myself. I took a long swallow from the bottle. It was a mistake. It brought the questions crowding in. With them came emotions I had no intention of dealing with that night, in that house, and if I could manage it, not ever.

Sidney came to the kitchen but I told him to leave me alone. I wasn't ready to talk to him. I woke in the morning, in bed, in my coat, shivering with cold, and Sidney woke with me. Daddy had told him about our conversation. That he wasn't my father, this had never occurred to Sidney, but he understood at once why I'd been treated with such coldness all my life. I think he understood.

—I don't want to talk about it, I said. You have to let me deal with this by myself. The best thing you can do is leave me alone.

—Are you coming back with us?

—I want to see Iris. I'll get the train.

We lay there in silence. Neither of us wished to leave the warmth of the bed. Through the gap in the drapes I could see the lowering gray sky outside. There was more snow on the way.

—Your father said you didn't want to know the circumstances.

—Did you hear what I said? And he's not my father.

—He was very upset.

What was he trying to do, effect a reconciliation? Fat chance.

—You're making me angry, I said.

He climbed out of bed and rapidly got dressed. He paused at the door and said he didn't think I should blame my sister. Then he left the bedroom. The effect of his words was to awaken the anger I'd intended to suppress. My family had lied to me all my life, this was how I saw it, so why should I care that the old man was upset? *I* was upset, *I, Constance!* I heard Sidney in the corridor with Howard. He wanted to get in bed with me again but Sidney told him he couldn't.

—Why not?

—She's upset.

Later I packed the boy's suitcase while Sidney gave him breakfast in the kitchen. I came down to see them off. I'd scraped my hair back off my forehead in a tight knot and I'd never before felt so distant or so very severe as I did then. Daddy looked exhausted. He hadn't slept. I was indifferent to him. I had a splinter of ice in my heart that morning, oh yes. I knew he was suffering. He'd handled it badly, and doubtless he was asking himself how you handle such a thing well. How do you break the silence of almost thirty years in a sensitive manner?

—When's Iris coming?

He'd just said good-bye to Sidney and Howard. I was with him in the kitchen. I was making fresh coffee. I didn't trouble to tell him when Iris was coming. Let him rot in hell.

I took the truck to the station. When I saw my sister on the platform I felt a brief pang of the old protective affection but I hated that she knew. A cold fury had raged inside me ever since Daddy told me. I'd thought: How could it not be Iris's fault that she'd kept it from me? She must have acquiesced in some notion of the old man's that it was for my own good. Then through perverse loyalty to him, or just sheer laziness, or carelessness, she'd failed me. Wasn't Iris more than a sister to me? Wasn't she my best friend? Hadn't I been a mother to her after Harriet died? But here she was, striding down the platform with a bag slung over her shoulder. She was in a dirty old fur coat she'd picked up second-hand in the city, it was flapping open, also velvet trousers tucked into a pair of ridiculous cowboy boots. She had a cigarette between her teeth and she was grinning.

—Hello, captain.

—Give me one of those.

She handed over the pack and clicked her lighter. Driving back to the house not once did I look at her. I'd decided the old man could tell her what had happened. When she was getting out of the truck she asked me if I was okay.

—What do you mean?

—I feel sad here too.

—You feel sad for Daddy?

—I guess so.

We went into the house. The old man emerged from the sitting room, carefully closing the door behind him. The long, flinty face grew soft, or as soft as flint gets. Here was Iris, home at last. How impatient he must be, I thought, to get her to himself and give her the bad news. And ask her please to sort it out. I left them to it. I went out through the kitchen and walked down to the river. I had Iris's cigarettes in my pocket. I smoked two of them on the dock and felt ill.

I reported all this to Sidney when I got back to New York. I told him I was grateful that he'd left me to deal with Daddy and Iris by myself. It was family business, I said, it didn't concern him, he was better off out of it. Of course it concerned him, he told me. Oh, I'd made him angry. If it concerned me then it concerned him, he said. What did I think it meant, being married?

—Please don't do this now, I said.

We were eating lunch in the dining room. Wintry sunlight drifted into the room and the city was quiet for once in its life. I'd come in from Penn Station late the previous evening and been too tired to talk. My mood had hardened overnight. Sidney set down his knife and fork.

—Listen to me, he said. This is a bad shock you've had and I want to help you make sense of it. So don't, please, say it doesn't concern me.

He wanted me to understand that we had to face it together. He said that this news had tipped my world upside down and

I wasn't strong enough to deal with it. I might wear a mask for others, he said, but with him I must express the confusion and pain I was feeling.

He then said that maybe it was a good thing, what had happened, because now there was a chance I could abandon Daddy and face the world like an adult.

—Do I have to tell you everything? I said.

—I'm your husband, so yes, Constance, you do. That's our deal.

So I told him that when I got back up to the house Iris was in the kitchen. She told me she didn't know what to say. I said that telling me what she knew would be a start. She was surprised. Hadn't Daddy told me? No, I said, Daddy hadn't told me anything.

We'd sat across the table staring at each other. I could hear the old man shuffling around somewhere above us.

—He didn't tell you *anything?* said Iris.

Again I told her no, and she asked me if I really wanted to know. I was suddenly filled with dread. I knew bad news was coming at me fast.

—He committed suicide.

—I'm sorry, said Sidney quietly.

He'd been afraid of this, he said. He'd hoped there was some way I could be shielded from it but there wasn't. He asked me how I'd handled it and I said I didn't handle it, that I was numb before it sank in. I'd asked Iris why he'd done it.

—That's all I know. Daddy wouldn't tell me his name.

I felt a gust of anger. Then I asked her how old I was when it happened.

—You weren't even *born*, darling!

As though that would make me feel better!

—So I never knew him? But why do you know this and I don't? Why was it a secret? Why was I never told?

Iris said that Daddy had told her not to say anything about it. She felt ashamed now. But he'd been so insistent.

—Yes, Iris, but why did he tell you that?

Yes, why? Now we were getting to it. The numbness was starting to wear off. Iris fell silent.

—What do you know?

Nothing.

—Iris, *why wasn't I told?*

—He said you weren't strong enough.

I'd felt a kind of wildness then, as though something was breaking loose inside of me and threatening to burst out in a flood of destructive rage. I'd risen from the kitchen table. I wanted to go upstairs and tell him what he'd done. Iris stood with her back to the door.

—Constance, wait, please—

—Why should I care what you think? You were in on it! You all were!

—I know—

Iris still had her back to the door. Suddenly I felt drained. I sat down at the table. I lit a cigarette then crushed it out.

—Who was he? No, you don't know, anyway I don't want to hear it from you.

Then I put my arms on the table and lay my head down and wept for a while, and Iris had the sense not to say anything or try to touch me.

The next day I returned to New York without making peace with either of them. They'd tried. The old man, Daddy—what else was I going to call him?—in his halting way repeated, when we were alone together, that he wanted me to know the truth before it was too late. It took some effort not to voice the clamor of angry responses that sprang to my lips and I pretended not to hear him. I waited for him to get up the courage to say why he'd done this to me but no, he couldn't. He sat at the kitchen table waiting for Iris to walk through the door. When she didn't he shuffled to his feet and left the room without another word.

Iris tried harder. She was dismayed by the chill that had sprung up between us. But any sympathy I may have felt for her, I crushed it out. I had no intention of letting her down easy. And when she looked at me in that imploring way I felt the anger rising and I didn't trouble to stem it. I was more hurt by my sister's complicity in Daddy's deception than anything else.

—We all washed up?

I was in the bedroom, packing. I was catching a train back to the city and Iris was driving me to the station. I didn't trouble to straighten up and turn around.

—I don't know, are we?

—I hate this, said Iris quietly. You don't even know if it's true.

I didn't respond to this. My mind was made up. It made sense of everything. Iris left the room, saying she'd be out in the truck when I was ready. I went downstairs. Daddy stood in the hall. He was angry now.

—Constance.

—*Daddy.*

—I'm very disappointed you won't try to see this from my point of view. I did what I thought was right.

—But you got it wrong, didn't you?

I was at the front door. In the driveway Iris sat in the truck with the engine running. She was resting her forehead on the steering wheel. I seized the old man's arm. I gripped it hard. I drew close to him so he wouldn't be in any doubt as to what I was telling him.

—*You've always hated me and now I know why. You bastard.*

I walked out to the truck and tossed my suitcase in the back and climbed in. As we drove along the river I saw tears suddenly spill down Iris's face and I was glad.

—You were glad, said Sidney.

—Yes, Sidney, I was glad!

I glared at him, my face pushed forward and my hands laid flat on the table. He moved to the chair beside me and I let him hold me for several minutes. Then I stood up from the table without looking at him. I left the room and went down the hall, then into the bedroom and closed the door quietly behind me.

★

It was grotesque, what Sidney proposed. My life had been devastated by a doctor and he wanted me to see a shrink. Even to suggest it—! The idea that he should hand me off in this way, commit me to the care of a *doctor*, it showed the limits of his imagination. I told him it would do more harm than good. Shrinks, doctors, I said, they do more damage than anyone. I was sick at what Daddy did to me. Why would I give myself over to a psychiatrist? Sidney said he understood. He said sometimes there's virtue in not knowing. I let him think it. He had to think something.

For several days after my return he didn't mention what had happened upstate. Then one night he apparently thought I might be receptive. As we sat at the kitchen table he suggested in a studiously offhand manner that my father was at an age when he wanted to get last things cleared away. It was a primal human need, he said, to put matters in order before a journey. He meant death. I'd been distracted earlier but hearing this I became at once alert and angry.

—Yes, but why didn't he figure out what it would do to me? And Sidney, *he's not my father.*

—Are you sure?

He wasn't sure. He didn't think the old man was reliable anymore.

—*Yes.*

We sat in silence. I'd cooked us a couple of steaks and opened a bottle of wine. Howard was asleep and Gladys had gone home.

—So what about Iris? he said.

—I don't know.

—I don't think you'll be estranged over this.

It was important to him that we not be estranged. He thought Iris was one of my very few sources of support and he didn't want me to lose her. Sidney liked Iris. He wanted to get her in bed. I think he felt he'd married the wrong sister but he was too repressed to do anything about it.

—Listen, I said, how many times have I said something about Daddy and Iris thought, Constance still doesn't know. It must have happened a thousand times. Her silence was an act of betrayal *every single time*.

—She's young to face a dilemma like that. Her father tells her one thing, her heart tells her another.

I shrugged.

—That's not my problem.

Then I said I didn't know what Iris could say to make it right, and it would have to come from Iris.

—It's not my responsibility, I said.

He let this pass. I grew bored. I was getting nowhere. I could see he wasn't on my side.

—Oh, let's not talk about it, I said. What's up with you?

He told me *The Conservative Heart* was still unfinished. He was rewriting it again. He showed perseverance, at least. He wasn't going to give up. He'd put too much time into it already. But why he thought that another year would solve his problems was a mystery to me. I knew this much about it, that he'd taken for his text those lines from Wordsworth: *Sweet is the lore which nature brings; / Our meddling intellect / Misshapes the beauteous forms of things; / We murder to dissect.*

I agreed with the sentiment, how could you not? But Sidney didn't, and this was the problem. He was working *against* the idea. Thinking murders nothing, he said. So why was he having so much trouble finishing the bloody thing, as he now referred to it?

But I wasn't in the mood for Sidney's knotty vexations. He sat turning the salt cellar in his fingers.

—Let's just get back to this business of yours, he said.

—Why?

I didn't like it. I'd told him I didn't want to talk about it anymore. It was making me anxious now. My memories of my childhood were a mess. I'd barely slept since it happened. What was the point? It was bad for me. When my emotional equilibrium is disturbed my skin shows a kind of reddish bruising around the eyes. Sidney told me once I was an occluded young woman, but that in the purely physical aspect of my being I was transparent. He said he hated to see these blemishes on my face.

—I can imagine how confused you are.

I knew he'd do this to me. Was he deliberately trying to make it worse? I got up and stood at the sink with my back to him.

—Don't you think we should talk about it? he said.

No. I did not. I felt like a block of crystal. One more tap of his hammer and I'd shatter into a thousand pieces. He then said I was in crisis and that I ignored it at my peril.

—If you won't talk to me, he said, I think you should see someone.

I fled. I locked myself in the bathroom and sat on the side of the tub with my hands on my knees and my head down. He'd started a voice going in my head and I'd been doing so well. He thought I was going mad. Why else did he want to take me to a psychiatrist? After a while I got control of my breathing. I washed my face in cold water and brushed my hair. I went back to the kitchen. He was clearing up the dinner things. I'd made him angry. He was like Daddy that way: If I defied him over the smallest thing I was a bad girl, willful and obstructive.

—It's a suggestion, he said. Think about it, Constance, that's all.

Then he told me he was my husband. I think it was supposed to remind me of my place in the order of things. Clearly a lowly place. I nodded. I was holding on for dear life. He'd almost undone me. Didn't he understand, I said, that that's what I wasn't going to do? I wasn't going to think about it and I was going to try never to talk about it again, and whatever he was thinking, I said, whatever chains of reasoning were unspooling in that big murdering intellect of his—I didn't want to know.

So he opened his hands, a gesture of submission.

—We'll leave it for now, he said. Here, give me a hug.

It had to be done. I stood there like a statue in marble while he put his arms around me. He rubbed his cheek against my hair. He kissed the places where my skin was red. Getting no response he stepped back.

—Constance, I'm your husband, he said again. Please remember that.

I wasn't a happy woman in the morning but what I'd most feared was that he'd insist on telling me about my real father, I mean this faceless man who'd committed suicide before I was even born. There were times, later, when I embraced that faceless man so comprehensively I felt him to be a living presence in the apartment. But right then I didn't want to know. I wasn't even interested in *why* I didn't want to know. I think I felt that it wasn't for Sidney or Iris or Daddy to tell me what I had to deal with.

For some days this remained my attitude. When I touched the wound the pain flared anew. I didn't seek out company: Instead after work I wandered the galleries of the Met. I liked the ancient Egyptians. Their artifacts and sarcophagi aroused in me a mood of unthinking tranquility and, more important, a silence that could last for hours. I felt that Daddy had turned my mind into a crypt.

In it he'd buried the truth about my father. Now the crypt had been opened but the truth hadn't set me free, the reverse.

Then one night when I was alone in the apartment I made an important discovery. I found I could begin to confront the one piece of information Iris had given me about my father.

I was taking a bath. There was a drop of blood in the water and it set off a string of associations. I got out of the tub. I sat at the kitchen table in my bathrobe smoking a cigarette. I had a towel wrapped around my head like a turban and I was sitting very still. I was absorbed by an idea that until that moment I'd suppressed, the idea, I mean, of a man in such anguish that suicide was the only way out. I began to feel pity for him. Then it seemed I'd never felt such pity for anybody ever in my life before.

Then I stopped. It was enough. I hadn't lost control. I hadn't been overwhelmed. Instead I'd made a first step but toward what I couldn't yet say. But I was no longer so frightened. I was in possession of a piece of my true history, this is what it felt like. I resolved to go on at my own halting pace until I'd reclaimed the whole. I thought that then *I* might be whole. Meanwhile I'd carry with me this fragile ghost, the shadowy outline of my father. Soon I heard what I imagined to be his voice and felt then that he was becoming mine, where before he'd belonged to Daddy and Sidney and the rest.

Life was a little easier after that. This ghost of mine, I couldn't call him a memory, didn't provoke grief but instead a sort of tenderness. When Sidney got back from Atlantic City he said he recognized a change in my mood. I knew that he knew more than I did about my father but it wasn't his knowledge I wanted. I didn't want to know what Daddy had told him. It would have gotten skewed in Daddy's telling. Daddy hated my father. So I didn't take Sidney into my confidence, not yet. Instead I continued to hold my father like a sort of egg inside myself. I was afraid that if I talked about him some contained essence would evaporate in the air and leave me again bereft and with nobody to talk to. All this had to be concealed from Sidney, of course. He said I'd had a nervous shock, that was how he described it. I told him again that what upset me was the deception, Iris's more than Daddy's because Iris I'd trusted.

He backed off for a while. One night I asked him if he knew how my father died. Daddy thought I wasn't strong enough to hear the truth. I was sure Sidney was asking himself the same question, I could see him thinking it. They were right: I wasn't strong enough, but he told me anyway because I asked him to. Sidney didn't believe in shielding people from the truth.

—He fell under a train.

—Oh no. Oh Christ.

I hadn't expected this. I don't know what I'd expected but not this. It was a bad shock. I felt sick. Silently we sat there. I didn't leave the room because I had to show him I was strong enough. I wasn't having it, this assumption of my weakness. They didn't assume Iris was weak. He said the driver of the locomotive didn't see him but he felt the impact.

—You want a drink?

I nodded. He made me a drink.

—It was suicide, wasn't it?

—I think so.

A thousand questions were swarming in my brain but the one I still avoided asking was, *Who was he?*

—Do you know where he's buried?

—He was cremated.

—There's no grave.

—No.

—Was he a handsome man?

—Yes, he was.

Of course he had no way of knowing this. He had no way of knowing any of it for sure, but he did know what I wanted to hear and he thought it couldn't do any harm.

—Sidney, was he a *criminal?*

—No.

A long silence here. Then at last I asked the only question that really mattered.

—What was his name?

Here it got complicated.

★

Later that night I woke up. I was angry with Daddy again. I started to cry. Sidney hadn't been asleep. He took me in his arms and held me until it passed. *He didn't know what hit him:* Where did those words come from, who said them? It was starting to torment me. I'd heard them spoken after Harriet's funeral. They'd made me sick and I felt sick now. What did it mean that a stray phrase associated with a secret from which I'd been excluded provoked nausea? I turned on the lamp beside the bed. He asked me what was wrong and I said it was time. He had to tell me.

We went to the kitchen. We sat at the table. I was in my silk bathrobe and my hair was loose. He later told me that the redness around my eyes made me look like a child who'd been crying and rubbed too hard at the tears she'd shed.

—Mildred Knapp has never once spoken to me about her husband, I said.

—Now you know why.

I became distracted. I was thinking about Harriet's predicament, stuck in that big house miles from anywhere, Daddy at the clinic or out on house calls all hours of the day and night, a cruel situation to put any woman in. So she'd found some comfort with Walter Knapp, and who could blame her? It was Daddy's fault. It's always the man's fault. He'd neglected her, just as he'd neglected me. I tried to remember if Mildred had ever mentioned our connection. Had she ever tried to see Walter in me? No. Mildred Knapp never even looked at me. I was surprised how calm I felt. I thought: I'm not Constance Schuyler Klein, I'm *Knapp*. I asked Sidney where he'd died. If there was no grave, if I couldn't visit his grave, I could at least visit the place where it happened. But Sidney didn't know. He said it was near Ravenswood but not on the property.

★

I was alone in the apartment one evening. I was again thinking about my father. Until I knew where he died he remained somehow adrift in space and time, and not at peace. Nobody cared about him. No one cherished his memory, no flowers were left, no words spoken. I heard someone knocking. Who shows up unannounced at ten at night? A wild idea flickered to life in my mind. I went to the door but I didn't open it.

—Who is it?

Silence. But someone or something was outside the door. There'd been a knocking. I'd heard it distinctly. With racing heart I asked again, louder this time. I am not a superstitious woman, but there are more things in heaven and earth—

—Who's there?

I *am* a superstitious woman—

—Your sister.

Relief. Disappointment. She knocked again. I feared what would happen if I let her in. I wasn't strong. I'd be overwhelmed. She knocked a third time.

—Iris, go away. Just fuck off, please.

—Let me in for a minute.

I was once her mother. I didn't have it in me. I waited for a few seconds more, then I opened the door an inch or two. I saw her as though for the first time. She was showing the ill effects of sustained drinking. Her eyes were watery, her cheeks were puffy. I was still angry with her but before I could stop her she'd pushed her way in and taken hold of my face, her fingers spread across my cheeks and her thumbs pressed into my jaw. We stood there in the doorway and I smelled the liquor on her breath. We were both tall women, tall, angry women. She slapped me on the cheek and walked into the sitting room and threw herself down on the chesterfield.

—So why didn't you call me?

—Iris, you have to make this right between us. I'm not going to.

She didn't hear me. She sprang up and crossed the room to the drinks table. Her hair was in copious disarray. She was wearing a man's tweed jacket and blue jeans, also those stupid cowboy boots. She asked me where the master was.

—Atlantic City.

—Wanna get stinko?

I knew what was happening. She was making it right between us. This was how she went about it. A normal explanation or even an apology was out of the question. Fortunately for her I didn't want to discuss it either. An hour later the talk was starting to get loose. Iris was sitting on the floor with her back against an armchair, rolling a cigarette. She wanted to know if I thought she should move to Vermont. It was a dumb idea. I told her she had to go to medical school. I asked her if she'd talked to Daddy about it.

—No.

—But that's why you went up there.

—I think he knows anyway. But listen, something's happened.

She lit her ragged cigarette then busied herself picking tobacco off her tongue. What was the matter with this family, I thought. Why were they incapable of telling me the truth?

—I think he's had a stroke.

She'd noticed it the morning after I left. He'd slept later than usual and when he came downstairs his speech was slurred. After a few hours it cleared up.

—What else?

—Tremor in the fingers of his left hand. That cleared up too. You know he hardly drinks at all now.

—So what does it mean?

—It might be dementia, first signs. It might be nothing.

Mildred Knapp was going to let her know if anything else occurred. I was skeptical. I thought it was a play for sympathy on Iris's part. Get me worried about the old man, I might forget I hated him. She'd always had his interest at heart, not mine. Then I thought: Did I cause that stroke? I didn't ask her. I wasn't going to confide in her. But she'd read my mind. She told me I was killing him.

—Don't be absurd, I said.

—Just come up with me for a night.

—Why?

—Clear the air.

—It's too soon.

—Then when?

—I don't know. Never.

—I'm going up for the weekend.

—I'm glad, Iris.

—So if you change your mind—

She was at the table, freshening her drink. I was afraid she was going to start talking about Eddie Castrol. I dreaded another maudlin session with her telling me how her love was like a tree. She sat down on the floor again, spilling whiskey on the rug. That night in the fall when I'd gone to the hotel by myself Eddie had told me about his daughter, and I'd seen a different man, I'd seen a father. I'd told him I was surprised Iris hadn't mentioned that he had a daughter. He said he'd never told her, but he thought I'd understand. I did understand. None of this could I say to Iris, of course. Fortunately she wasn't finished with Daddy yet and I was spared a dirge. A little later she decided she loved me after all. She lifted high her glass and I poured her more scotch. I wanted her drunk. I wanted no more tricky questions and no soggy rambling.

—To life.

—Yeah.

She left soon after that and I gave her the cab fare to get downtown. I went back into the sitting room. I was still preoccupied with the glimpse I'd had, when she'd first knocked on the door, of the visitor I'd imagined waiting out there in the hallway.

She called me from upstate two days later. I asked her what was wrong. There was nothing wrong, she said, she just wanted to hear my voice. I stood at the window in my office as the rain came streaming down. The skyscrapers all around me were lost in mist. Their lights were mere bleary smudges in a kind of damp gauze and I felt that I was high in the mountains of that dreamy German painting, Sidney would know the artist. I let her tell me what she was doing. Not much, it was clear. She was bored. There was snow on the ground. Daddy's tremor had returned but not the slur. Mildred said he'd forgotten her name a few days earlier. I thought of how he'd made us stay in a cold house at Christmas. That was part of it, an early sign. And him telling me he wasn't my father, that was another.

—He talks about you all the time, she said.

—Oh sure.

She knew not to labor the point. If Daddy was in pain I felt no obligation to give him comfort. She did, but she loved him. Anyway she was a better woman than I. She was a more *messy* woman than I, with her drinking and her men and her feckless abandonment of a career in medicine, but she had a big heart and I didn't. It matters. Iris didn't have to make an effort at sympathy or warmth or generosity, it came naturally. It takes courage to stay receptive like that. It's much easier to *sour*. All the world's a *sour*. But now at least I knew who my father was.

★

I'd become obsessed with this one question. I wanted to know where he'd died. It was so I could let him rest in peace. I'd had the idea he was knocking on my door the night Iris came. He wasn't there, of course, I wasn't mad yet, but what the idea represented, what it *meant*, was that I had to let him in. I owed him more than I'd yet admitted, out of fear of being overwhelmed. I talked to Sidney again. I asked him why he fell under a train. We were in the kitchen. It was again late at night, it seemed the proper time to talk about these things. I remember being aware of the ticking clock above the stove, the apartment otherwise silent. I heard the hum of the refrigerator, and outside, a city bus starting up. I felt as though we were the only two people awake in all of Manhattan.

—Shame.

But what was he ashamed of? Sidney was evasive. He was like a lawyer now. He said that Daddy could no longer give reliable testimony about the past.

—I think he accused him of something, he said at last.

He reached across the table for my hand. I didn't want to be touched. I just wanted to know what happened.

—He said he attacked your mother.

I pushed my chair back and went to the window. I spoke without turning around.

—Sexually?

—Yes.

I didn't believe it. This was Daddy's doing. I asked Sidney if he thought Daddy was telling the truth.

—Do you? he said.

I turned to face him. I was furious suddenly. I remember I stood glaring at him, leaning forward a little, with my arms folded tight across my chest. There couldn't be any doubt about it. It was an ugly, contemptible lie. I saw no reason to think Harriet was coerced, nor would I accept that I was a child of rape, if that's what he was telling me. After a while I came back to the table.

—How did he find out? I said.

—Mildred.

—If Harriet was raped she'd have told him herself.

—Perhaps.

He stayed quiet. He let me think it through. It seemed normal to be sitting in the kitchen at dead of night talking like this. A moment later it was all very bizarre and disquieting.

—So did he actually *say* my father killed himself out of shame?

—I couldn't get a straight answer out of him. I said he had to tell me for your sake but he was vague. I think he may have told him he'd be prosecuted and that's what—

—That he'd go to prison.

—He'd go to prison. It wouldn't look good for him, not if it was his word against the doctor's. Not unless your mother—

He didn't want to finish his sentences. He wanted me to put it together for myself. But it was too much for me then. I was suddenly exhausted. I could barely stay awake. He followed me into the bedroom and within seconds I was asleep.

Later he said he believed Daddy was trying to tell him what happened, but that frailty of memory and, too, some residual moral revulsion had confused the thing in the old man's mind.

—It's tragic, he said. Your whole life all you've wanted is your father's love. Then you discover he isn't your father at all, and your real father died before you were even born.

All my life I'd been building on quicksand, was that what he was telling me? Unspoken was the question whether I had the resilience to sustain this fresh damage. Daddy threatened my father. He told him he'd go to jail for what he'd done. So my father threw himself under a train. Why couldn't Sidney grasp the obvious here? *Daddy was responsible.*

SIX

HE TOOK ME to Penn Station. He didn't want me to go to Ravenswood without him but he wasn't free. There were no cabs so we had to take the subway. We were crushed together among damp irritable New Yorkers hanging on to leather straps being jolted to and fro with every jerk and judder of the train. It was slow and noisy. There was much screaming and grinding of metal on metal. Electricity sparked and flared in black tunnels. It was filthy, too, trash on the floor and graffiti smeared all over the doors and windows. Penn Station was worse. The work of demolition continued unabated, hammers clanging on girders, the roar of heavy machinery, men shouting. It was too much for me. Coils and wires spilling out of walls. The concourse had already been gutted and there was a crane in there now, and almost as bad as the noise was the dust. It got in your eyes, your lungs, your stomach. Sidney said we were being forced to eat Penn Station as a punishment for letting it die. I thought, the hell with Penn Station, who let my father die?

A week had passed. Iris had visited Daddy and returned to the city. Now it was my turn. I'd told Sidney I had to go see the old man because apparently I was killing him. I said I wanted to be around for his last words. I hoped they'd be: *Forgive me.*

—And you'd say?

He told me he hated how bitter I'd become. He said he wanted his sweet innocent girl back. I said that Daddy had destroyed my innocence by telling me the truth.

—I'd say, forget it!

I told him I just wanted the chance to say good-bye to it all: I wanted a last look at what I was about to lose forever. I said I intended never to return after this visit, it was just to lay a ghost. That wasn't so far from the truth. I had to find out where he died. I owed it to him. It was the least I could do.

North of Cold Spring there was a fierce chill and the river was icy silver beneath a cloudless sky. I had a manuscript with me and I worked for most of the journey. I left the train at Rhinecliff and found a cab in the station yard. I had the driver take the river road. By the time we turned in to the driveway I was making a conscious effort to keep my breathing steady. I hadn't called in advance.

I knocked on the front door then stood on the porch for more than a minute. Snow still blanketed the roof and clung to the slates of the tower. Icicles hung frozen from the eaves and there was frost in the upstairs windows. It was like a kind of ice museum, or a mausoleum, or a *sarcophagus*, and I thought, More than Harriet's spirit left this house when she died. There's no heart here anymore. There hasn't been for years. I wanted very badly to turn around and go straight back to New York.

But there were signs of life. Firewood was stacked on the verandah and the stack was much depleted since Christmas. Wood
smoke drifted from a chimney. Tools were propped in the porch,
an ax, a saw, and a hatchet. They should have gone back to the
barn. Daddy got furious when tools were left out. And the truck
was out front although it looked as if it hadn't been driven in a
while. Then the front door opened and Mildred Knapp stood
there wiping her hands on her apron. This woman was married to
my father. I stared at her with new eyes. I don't know what I
expected to see. She saw nothing.

—He didn't say you were coming.

Blunt and chilly as ever.

—I didn't tell him.

The house wasn't warm. I followed her across the hall and down
the corridor. I felt oddly exhilarated, knowing that she didn't know
that I knew who I was. If she did know she gave no sign of it. I
tried to find something in her I'd missed before, some kind of
connective tissue. Some *link*. I left my bag at the foot of the back
stairs and went into the kitchen. She stood at the counter and
poured me a cup of coffee.

—Iris is worried about Daddy, I said.

—Most days he's like he always was.

She put the cup of coffee in front of me. She was a woman of
sinew, lean and weathered in her frame and in her hands, and with
a harsh, bony face. The untidy black hair was threaded with silver.
She'd moved into the tower soon after Harriet died and she lived
up there still, alone with her memories and her secrets. She was my
father's wife but not a word of it had ever passed between us. She

was another one who'd kept the truth from me. To her too I was the living embodiment of betrayal. They both hated me. It made no sense. None of us controls the circumstances of our birth. It doesn't take much imagination to figure that out.

—He doesn't want to get out of bed. He says it's too cold. Imagine that, your father afraid of cold weather. He'll get up when he knows you're here.

Your father.

—You think you should tell him?

—It's better if I go up.

She left the kitchen and I thought no, maybe she doesn't hate me. If she thinks about me at all it's in connection with Daddy's welfare. The rest belongs in some archive in her mind stocked with ancient scandals. She visits them at night, then at dawn she locks them away again. She returned to the kitchen a few minutes later.

—He'll be down soon, she said. It takes him a while, getting washed and dressed.

—You see a big change.

—Like I said, some days he's himself.

She did something with her face then, a sucking in of the lower lip and a biting down on it, producing a tight pucker round the mouth that to me suggested pain. She loved him in her way. For years he'd looked after her sisters and their children. To her he was a good man. He was the doctor. She hated to see him grow weak. Then I heard his step on the stair, descending.

The change was not as dramatic as I'd been led to expect. He stood in the kitchen doorway much as I remembered him at Christmas, looming and frowning in his cardigan and corduroys.

He was thinner than before. There was a prickle of white stubble on his jaw. There was a tremor in his left hand. But more remark- able was what occurred next.

—Morgan, shut the door, said Mildred sharply, you're letting the heat out.

He entered the kitchen and closed the door behind him. His docility astonished me. It wouldn't have happened like this even a month before.

—You didn't tell us, Constance. We didn't know you were coming.

—It was spur of the moment. Is it all right?

He shuffled toward the table and in his gait I saw an old man. He spoke to the floor in a querulous tone. He reached with trem- bling hand for the chair at the end of the table. Carefully he sat down.

—Is it all right, she asks me, is there anything to be done about it now? I don't think so.

His head lifted.

—Mildred, give me a cup of coffee.

Later when we were alone I told him I knew who my father was.

—Oh you do.

We were in the sitting room by the fire. It was getting dark outside.

—Who told you?

—Not you.

He nodded to himself for a while. I'd always avoided confront- ing him if I could. He was too strong for me. Now I had no choice.

—I thought it might be too much for you, he said.

—You wanted me to think you were my father.

He answered without hesitation. I knew the tone and I hated it. I was angry with myself for having elicited it. It was the clinical tone, and he used it when he spoke of matters about which he felt certain. He told me that yes, he did want that, it was better that way—

He sank back in his chair. I went to the window. I pulled the drapes closed. Away from the fireplace the room was cold but I had to put some distance between us. I asked him why he'd told me at all.

Again the bowed head.

—Daddy, *why?*

He spread his old hands, palms upward. There was no tremor.

—You have Sidney now.

—Sidney said you told Walter Knapp he'd go to jail and that's why he killed himself.

He waved this away with weary disdain.

—That boy disrupted the household and I had to get rid of him.

—What do you mean?

—I mean I crushed him.

He lifted his hand and rubbed his thumb against his fingertips. I was standing over him now.

—What are you saying?

He sat back in the chair with his eyes closed.

—Sit down, he said quietly.

I stood there, staring down at him, aghast.

—Sit!

I obeyed him.

—I found them together in the damn boathouse.

—What were they doing?

He was silent.

—Daddy, what were they doing?

Blood from a stone! He opened his pale eyes. They were spark-
ing with contempt. He asked me what I thought they were doing.
But I needed to hear him say it! I had to know that this part of it
at least was true.

—What did you do?

He shook his head. I felt as though I was trapped in a nightmare,
the horror of it the persisting sensation of not being asleep.

—So they were in the boathouse—

—Where you were forbidden to go! I put a lock on it to keep
you out but you paid no attention to that, did you, you and your
sister? Now do you understand why I didn't want you in there?

There was nobody else in the house except Mildred, and she'd
already gone to the tower. Was he telling me he murdered my
father in the boathouse? That that's how he died? I asked him what
happened when he found them.

He was groping in the pocket of his jacket. He produced a small
object. It glinted in the firelight. He held it out for me to see. It
was a thin, scratched silver ring. Whose ring? He wouldn't say.
Walter's, I thought. He'd taken it from his body, he'd pulled it
from his finger. He'd kept it as a kind of memento mori.

—Here, have it, he said.

When I was a child, and they were talking, Daddy and
Harriet, and I came into the room, they'd fall silent and I

thought they were talking about me. But I knew now they were talking about my father. That Daddy wouldn't let it go, that he continued to punish Harriet to the end of her life. That he'd caused her death too.

—At least tell me where he died.

But he was indifferent to me now. I wasn't his daughter, I was nothing to him. He was panting slightly. I saw him as monstrous.

—I know how you did it, I said. I know what you said to him.

—You know nothing.

He rose to his feet and I followed him to the kitchen. He was exhausted. Spittle was flecked on his lips and chin. His skin was ashen. It was wearing him out, all this drama I'd brought into the house. After we'd eaten he said he was going to bed. There was some clumsy pushing back of the chair as he got up from the table. I stood up and carefully put my arms around him. He allowed himself to be held and then he shuffled to the door. He paused, and turned, and I waited for the words that would shed light on what had just transpired, or at least affirm that love had once existed between us, and perhaps still did, and I asked myself: Is that why I've come here? Because it was no good trying to get the truth out of him. He was too old, and for old men there's no point, there's no past, there's only the future, and it bears down on them with inexorable purpose: death in the form of the Albany train, or whatever instrument of termination it chooses for its work—

He told me to be sure the screen was on the fire before I went to bed.

After he'd gone upstairs I got my coat on and left the house by the back door. It had started to snow. I made my way down the hill and across the tracks. The snow came drifting in moist heavy flakes. I stood at the end of the broken dock and watched it melting in the icy water where it lapped at the pilings beneath my feet. Then I turned to the boathouse.

I pushed open the slatted doors. I remembered it as a summer place full of moving shadows and watery echoes, sunlight shafting through gaps in the planks, but that winter night it was dark, and where before it had been romantic now it was sinister. Daddy's boat was tightly battened under its canvas canopy, green with lichen. The skiff was gone but he'd removed the outboard before he scuttled it and there it still was, clamped to a sawhorse and covered with a tarpaulin. Was it here?

I began to shiver. I felt sick. Then I was pulling the doors closed behind me. High on the bluff above me reared the black mass of the house. Its outline was sharp in definition in the falling snow.

When I returned to the city I told Sidney that Daddy killed my father. But Sidney didn't take me seriously. He tried to tell me that the old man's grasp of past events was not reliable, surely that was apparent to me. I couldn't hold the old man responsible for this ancient tragedy.

I'd been afraid of this. I bowed my head and covered my face with my hands. Then I looked up at him.

—You said you were on my side, I said quietly. It wasn't a tragedy, Sidney. It was murder. And it wasn't Daddy who told me.

—Then who did?

—Mildred.

He said he had no more confidence in Mildred Knapp's version of events than he did in Daddy's.

—Did she see him do it?

—She didn't have to.

—No?

—No, Sidney, she didn't. She's been living with him since Harriet died. She shares his bed, or she used to.

I told him that in the morning after my conversation with Daddy I'd risen early and gone downstairs to the kitchen and found Mildred at the sink washing the dishes. I told her that Daddy and I had talked about Walter. I told her I knew he was my father. She didn't turn around. She didn't move.

—And does he know you know? she said at last.

—Yes.

Then she'd turned. We stared at each other for several seconds.

—Where did he die? I said.

My heart was racing. I knew she'd tell me.

—South of here.

—How far?

—Tillman's Landing.

I felt a rush of anguished recognition. I cried out. I remembered Tillman's Landing. A riverside hamlet, four or five houses and a dock. A steep dirt track off the river road that ended at the water. Mildred sat down at the table. She reached across and seized my hand.

—I tried to stop him, she whispered.

—What do you mean?

But she was alarmed now. She couldn't do it. She pulled away from me. She got up from the table. Then she was standing at the sink with her back to me, furiously pumping water into a saucepan. Our moment of intimacy had vanished as fast as it came.

—Do you have any photographs of him?

—I burned them all!

—What was he like?

Mildred still didn't turn around. Her thin back was taut with tension under a cheap black cardigan.

—Ask him, he knows.

She meant Daddy.

—He won't tell me.

She shrugged. She was a cruel woman, or perhaps she was just a frightened woman, or a guilty woman. I lost patience with her. I was weeping now. I took the keys from the hook by the telephone and got my coat on. I went out to the truck. It was parked by the barn. I climbed in and drove away. I heard a shout from behind me. In the mirror I saw Mildred on the front porch. She was pulling on her overcoat and running down the steps. I backed up. She got in beside me. I had no idea where I was going but then I realized I did know, I was going south on the river road. I was going to Tillman's Landing and Mildred was coming with me.

The river was placid that day, slow moving, full of ice, silver in places beneath a gray wintry sky. I began to breathe more easily. I loved its steady beauty. I loved its calm. We drove in silence.

Tillman's Landing was as I remembered it. Nothing had changed here. The road was unpaved and I followed it round a wooded headland and then it opened below us, the cluster of roofs, the railroad tracks and the dock, the station house, boarded up now, whitewash flaking off the bricks, and beyond it the silvering river and the distant mountains under a lowering leaden sky. Telephone poles marched along the railroad tracks. There was nobody around. On the high ground to the south leafless trees stood stark against the sky. I was strongly aware of my father's presence, or no, not his presence, his *influence*.

I drove down the hill and parked the truck. We sat staring at the railroad tracks and the river beyond.

—Was it here? I said.

Mildred nodded.

—So what happened?

Something happened. Something brought it to a head. Daddy got suspicious. He got wind of it. Perhaps he came home from work unexpectedly in the middle of the day, or they did something reckless and he saw it. All Mildred would tell me at first was that he found them in the boathouse.

—Where were you? I said.

She was in the tower. She saw Daddy going down to the boathouse. Then Walter came out. He went along the railroad tracks and Daddy followed him. A little later Harriet left the boathouse and came back up through the woods. She reached the house and went upstairs to her bedroom. Mildred stood outside her door and heard her crying. She was glad.

—You were glad, I said.

—I thought that was the end of it.

—But it wasn't?

—It was the end of it all right.

What she meant was, the very thing happened that she'd been afraid of. She never got him back. A few hours later they told her he'd been hit by the Albany train.

128

It cost her, saying this. She became distraught. She took a few minutes to compose herself. Then she was pointing at the tracks where a low wooden platform allowed vehicles to pass over the rails to the towpath. That's where he died, she said.

My father.

—Why did he do it?

She glanced at me and then looked away. She puckered her mouth like she had the day before. Then she started to talk. We sat in the truck for an hour and not a living soul emerged from any of the houses, the place was empty, it was dead. Not even a train.

She was young when she married Walter, she said, they were both young. Her sisters were all against it. They'd heard stories about him. I wanted to know what the stories were, I wanted to know everything. What was he like? He was like you, she said.

—How like me?

He had my coloring, very fair-skinned, she said, and his hair was like yours, almost white. A strange boy. He heard things, like you do, and he'd get distracted. He'd get lost in his thoughts. You never knew for sure what he was feeling, he kept it to himself. He wrote things and sometimes he'd read them to me. What were they about? Oh, the river. The woods. Me, she whispered. But when he was happy . . . When he was happy the sun came out—

She smiled a little. She'd loved him of course.

So it was small things we had in common, she said, but they alarmed her. She'd think, Where did that come from? She found it uncanny we were so similar. It had unsettled her. I thought, She must have felt I was accusing her, but of what I didn't know. Of not saving him. All these years I'd kept her misery alive, that was why she hated me. After they were married they'd moved into the servants' rooms at the back of the house and he was taken on as a groundsman. The place was kept up to a higher standard then. There was more money, more staff. There were dogs and horses. They threw parties. People came up from the city.

She fell silent. She was gazing through the windshield at the railroad tracks. I told her I never knew the house in those days, it was before I was born. She said it was all coming to an end even before Walter died. No money, she said. The doctor had to take on more patients. She didn't know what happened but there was some disaster and then there was no money anymore. She thought it was Harriet's money they lost. The doctor was out all hours of the day and night. Your mother was bored. She'd wander around the house with nothing to do. She'd never got along with the local people. She'd known a different life, growing up in England. There were times she helped Mildred in the kitchen just to make work for herself. In the summer she'd always be in the garden. She got frustrated because it wasn't like an English garden. The soil was poor and the season was short so she couldn't grow the things she wanted to. Walter helped her with the garden and that's how it started.

—How did it start, Mildred?

It was like she'd just bitten into a lemon, the taste in her mouth was so bitter. I grew up here, she said, but your mother, oh, your mother, she was different. She was *English*. But we got along fine at first. Then she took a liking to Walter.

Another long pause.

—I began to suspect something, she said at last.

She fell silent again.

—Go on, I said. You started to suspect something.

She wiped her eyes. She began to speak again but without looking at me now.

—It got bad in the house after that.

—Okay.

I wasn't surprised. Harriet wouldn't be satisfied by a cold man like Daddy. He'd never be enough for her, not in that way. Mildred was staring at the tracks again and it was her sour face I saw, the face I'd known all my life. Walter and Harriet between them made that face. Walter wouldn't talk to her about what was going on but it had become obvious. How? I couldn't find them, she said. They'd disappear. I knew they'd gone off together. Then later there'd be looks between them. It made me sick. I couldn't be around them.

She was sure they talked about going away together—those two! Your mother, she said, running off with Walter Knapp!

I didn't see what was so strange about that.

—What about Daddy? I said.

—I couldn't tell him. How could I tell him?

—He didn't see it for himself?

—He wasn't here during the day. At night he'd drink whiskey and then go to bed. It wasn't much of a marriage even before your mother started up with Walter.

There was silence for a while in the cab of the truck. It had all played out over one summer, when they could meet out of doors, find places in the woods or elsewhere on the property like the boathouse. She started to buy him gifts. Mildred found them, a

131

silver cigarette case, a ring. Books. She'd have given him anything, she said. She thought Harriet had demeaned herself. Walter was good enough for Mildred, oh yes, she'd have made a good life for the two of them, she'd have looked after him, better than Harriet ever could.

—I didn't blame him so much, she said. I couldn't expect him to just ignore your mother, it wasn't in his nature. He was like a leaf in the wind that way. But for her to then bring *love* into it—

This was what excited her deepest scorn. Harriet brought love into it. In Mildred's eyes it made it all so much worse. In mine it was the only thing that mattered.

—Then he died and it wasn't an accident, was it?

He died for love but Mildred couldn't see that. She shook her head. She didn't speak for a few minutes. She covered her face with her hands. Then it came out, what Daddy had said to Walter. He told him he'd make sure he was sent to prison for a very long time. He said he could make that happen and Walter believed him, although I think he was distraught not so much about going to prison but because he'd lose Harriet. But he'd lost her already! That was the worst of it, that it was over once it was discovered. Walter thought he had a choice but it was no choice at all, and Mildred said it was all just an illusion, that Harriet had convinced him to believe some foolish illusion and he thought he couldn't leave her.

—If he'd just come to me—

She shook her head again. She couldn't afford even to consider the possibility that they were in love.

—He decided there was only one way out, she said.

—Did Daddy know that?

—He suggested it.

Mildred now told me she *had* been in the boathouse that day. She'd followed Daddy and tried to stop him going in, but there was no chance of that. He was very angry. But what he found he hadn't expected. Walter had torn his hand on a nail. He was sitting on the planks in the sunlight, by the water, and Harriet was kneeling over him, dabbing at the cut with a wet handkerchief. She looked up when Daddy came in. She didn't seem surprised. She told him he should be doing this, she meant looking after Walter's hand.

—Get out, said Daddy.

Walter was in some pain. It was a deep cut and there was blood all over Harriet's dress.

—You can't stop us, he said.

—Shut up, said Harriet.

—Get out, said Daddy again.

—Oh Morgan, said Harriet, don't be tiresome.

Mildred glanced at me, as though to say: You believe this? How she behaved? Walter stood up. He was clutching her handkerchief to his palm.

—I love her, he said.

Mildred turned to me. I thought she was going to cry.

—Go on, I said.

So then Walter walked slowly out of the boathouse, she said. *He didn't even look at me.* Daddy followed him. They went south along the tracks in single file. I could see them, two ghostly figures in the mist. I was becoming distressed by this point.

133

Mildred asked me if I was strong enough for the rest. Oh, I was strong enough. I saw it all clearly now. I saw Walter at Tillman's Landing with his bleeding hand, sitting on the ground against the station-house wall, facing the tracks. Daddy was crouching close beside him with his long back bent, a hand on the boy's shoulder. His pale eyes were hooded as he described in a whisper a woman pacing her bedroom, beside herself with the terror of exposure, of being on display, the prospect of the thing coming out in open court—

—You want that, Walter? You want her to go through all that?

Then up comes Daddy's head as the Albany train is heard approaching, the clanging of its bell. Here, now, he whispers, do it now, Walter, I'll be with you. And he reaches down to my father, who then rises to his feet, and together they walk toward the tracks as the train comes into view, hand in hand like father and son—

Silence in the cab of the truck.

—He didn't care about Walter, said Mildred at last, it wasn't him he was angry at. It was her. He wanted to hurt her. He told me so himself. He said he was tired of feeling humiliated. That's why he made Walter do it, he wanted to punish her. No other reason.

—And afterward? I said quietly.

—Oh afterward, she said. He felt sorry about it afterward, but she never forgave him. He tried to make it right between them but she wouldn't listen. Not even when Iris was born. Not even when she was dying.

She paused.

—And for you it was already too late, she said.

—What do you mean?

—She was pregnant.

★

Back in the city that night I reflected on what had been done to me, or no, not what was done to me but what was *withheld*, what was *denied*, what was *still* denied. It wasn't just Daddy, it was Sidney too, because he excused him, he defended him, and having told me the truth he then denied it, and I couldn't seem to just *shut my feelings down*. So much better to be numb, I thought. To be dead inside. To be blind, to be deaf, yes, above all to be deaf. Better the bulwarks—

Sidney was going out of town for two days. He asked me if I wanted him to cancel his trip. No, I told him. I'm all right, I said. He left in the morning and he took Howard with him. That night I went to the Dunmore Hotel. I wanted to hear Eddie Castrol play the piano.

SEVEN

I WON'T FORGET those somber drives Howard and I took to Atlantic City that winter when we talked of all manner of things both grave and trivial but without ever forgetting the dying woman at the end of our journey. Wry, weary, in some pain, apparently resigned to an early death but comforted by the presence of her son and sustained by the salty candor of her mother, Barb bore her illness with fortitude and humor. But she distracted me from Constance and this was not good. After her last visit to her father's house she'd been distant and impenetrable. She no longer trusted me because I was skeptical about the story she'd heard from Mildred Knapp. She said I was on *his* side, *he* being Daddy. Several times I tried to talk to her about it but it did no good. Her mind was made up. So I left her alone. I told her I'd be there when she needed me.

But I was stretched too thin just then and I didn't understand how precarious her situation had become. One day in February a call came from Iris. She'd gone back up to Ravenswood. She had bad news, she said.

—Tell me, I said.

—He's had another stroke. I don't know what to do.

I left the city early the next morning, alone. Howard was staying with his grandmother in Atlantic City. My sense of dread deepened the farther north I got. It was a bleak, chill, late-winter landscape. The trees were bare and there was snow on the ground. I arrived at the house. I sat at the kitchen table and Iris told me what had happened since she got here. There was one morning, she said, when he'd appeared in the kitchen saying that thieves had been in the house. They'd stolen his watch and his hairbrush. He wanted to call the police but Mildred dissuaded him. Then he wanted to drive into the village, but he couldn't find the truck keys. Mildred had had to hide them.

The next morning I sat in the office of Morgan's doctor, a serious young man in horn-rim spectacles called Hugo Friedrich. He'd taken over the practice some years before. I asked him if Dr. Schuyler should be in a nursing home.

—I wouldn't envy you, trying to move Morgan Schuyler out of his own house, he said. His tone was sardonic. He paused. In terms of treatment, he then said, I have nothing to offer you.

—How long has he got?

—One year, maybe two. Maybe seven.

He gazed at me impassively. He seemed almost to relish his inadequacy in the face of this disease. I asked him to please make another house call.

—He wouldn't see me the last time.

—I'm sure you understand the sort of man he is.

—Yes, I know what sort of man he is.

—And you won't allow your antagonism to interfere with your clinical duties.

I'd gone too far.

—Professor Klein, he said, please don't tell me my clinical duties. I'm saying that I'm no use to you if I can't get into the patient's bedroom. Yes, I'll try.

He stood up. The interview was over. But he had to know what was expected of him. When Iris went back to the city, Mildred Knapp would need all the help she could get from this doctor.

I was in the kitchen with Iris when the old man appeared in the doorway.

—I've been asleep, he said.

—You had a good sleep, said Iris.

—Not good enough. I woke up.

This was how he talked now. It was a lousy sleep because he woke up. He'd changed. He was a sick man. It diminished him. He sat at the table and asked for a glass of wine. When it was put in front of him he stared at it and I saw the life drain out of his face. His eyes died and his features grew slack. His mouth fell open. It was as though all meaning had fled from him. He knew the meaning of nothing and had no meaning himself. There was emptiness where the old man sat. Iris looked at me and shook her head. Don't even try, she seemed to be saying.

It lasted forty minutes. Then he came back to life. He reached for his wine. His hand was unsteady. It cost him everything he had to pull himself out of it, whatever black trough he'd been sunk in. There'd been an absence of affect, cognition, will: self, in short. Now he was attempting to make conversation. It was harrowing to watch. A little later I went out and made my way down through the trees to the river. Sticks and other debris drifted by on the current. The water was flat calm. To the north the delicate arch of the Kingston Bridge floated in the twilight like a sketch in charcoal on gray paper. Beyond it the Catskill ridges were blue against the dusk. We seemed to be approaching the end of something, some phase of life, and I hoped to Christ it wasn't my marriage. I felt sure I'd been wrong to leave Constance by herself in the city.

Oh what can ail thee, wretched wight, / Alone and palely loitering . . .

Yes, and palely loitering I watched the river grow molten and then flush red as the sun went down behind the mountains. A flock of geese flapped low across the water, which turned pale as ice, elsewhere suffused with the fire of the dying sun. When the Albany train went through it was with a great clangor of bells. Then I saw Iris picking her way down through the trees, her fur coat flapping open and a cigarette between her teeth.

She sat beside me on the dock. As her father's condition deteriorated she became more dispirited, this hadn't escaped me. But still I heard the compassion in her voice as she spoke of finding him stooped and fearful in the kitchen door when she'd first arrived at the house. The corridor was dark and at the far end he stood half turned toward her with one hand lifted. She'd dropped her bag at the foot of the stairs and gone forward. He'd started to retreat into the kitchen. His hand was still lifted to ward her off as though she were a stranger come to do him harm. It shocked her that he didn't know who she was.

She then told me he'd had the second stroke the day Constance returned to the city. Did I know what Constance had said to him? I didn't. She became a little tearful. He was old and sick and Constance should just leave him in peace, she said. She should leave him alone. I was again struck by their difference in temperament. Clear emotional currents flowed close to the surface in Iris and they were easy to read. Constance's feelings were so tortuous, by contrast, and so veiled, so complicated, that I felt exhausted even thinking about her. A small wave rolled in from somewhere out in the river and broke gently against the pilings. We felt the dock shift beneath us. It wasn't safe.

—How still it is, Iris whispered.

A few moments later she was silently weeping. When I touched her shoulder the grief all at once poured out of her and she cried like a child, rocking back and forth on the deck. I put my arms around her and held her. It was like a summer shower, very sudden and intense. Then it was over. I asked her what that was all about.

—Oh who knows, she said, groping for a cigarette.

I suspected it wasn't only her father's decline that troubled her. There was a man in the city and her heart had been broken, this much I knew but no more. I told her she was too young for all this sorrow.

Late that night she came down to the kitchen and found me there. She said she couldn't sleep either. She sat beside me on the old bench by the woodstove. I put my book down. She thanked me for being kind to her earlier. Her eyes were red and her mascara was smudged. Her feet were bare on the cold stone floor and that lovely heap of blonde hair was tumbled about her shoulders. She sat beside me and gazed at me with an expression of wry sad humor.

—Did she tell you about Eddie? she said.

★

I returned to the city in the morning. I encountered only light traffic but by the time I could see the George Washington Bridge I was going at a crawl. There were shrieking car horns and gas fumes and rage. I was tired. I thought of that senile old man and all he was accused of and I tried to organize it into some kind of a story. Those two women, each one damaged, each one desperate because of him, Iris no less than Constance. I couldn't seem to do it. I felt the same frustration when I tried to see the city with any clarity now, for it too defied comprehension in its current state of entropic dissolution, by which I mean *decay. Breakdown.* An idea occurred to me. I glimpsed the title of my next book, the one I'd write once I'd laid aside the bloody albatross, my *Conservative Heart.* Why that book defied all my efforts to finish it I didn't know. But this new one, it would be called *A Scream in the Night.* It would be a psychosocial study of urban breakdown, the collapse of a great American city. It would be a damn sight easier, I thought, to explain what was happening to New York City than to figure out what was going on in my wife's psyche.

Hours later I turned onto West Sixty-ninth and parked the Jag. I went up in the elevator. I unlocked the door. The apartment was dark. I felt uneasy. I left my suitcase in the hall. The sitting room door was closed. Quietly I opened it. She was at the window, staring out, talking on the phone. The room was dark. No lamps had been lit. She didn't hear me. She thought she was alone. I heard her tell someone she had just one question and then she'd never mention it again.

—Do you still love her?

I couldn't of course hear the reply. I imagine he said, Who?

—You know who, you fool. My sister.

The response, perhaps: I'm with her now.

—Don't torment me. When do you finish?

He didn't answer. The line went dead. She must have thought somebody had come into the room he was speaking from. She turned from the window. But no, somebody had come into the room *she* was speaking from. She was visibly startled: I was sitting in an armchair, watching her.

—I didn't hear you come in.

—Was that Eddie?

She walked to the table. She turned on the lamp. She'd changed. There was a kind of *poise* I'd never seen in her before, a practiced ease. She was acting. I'd surprised her. But how much had I overheard? She replayed the conversation in her head, I saw her doing it. How transparent she was. She heard herself say: *Don't torment me.*

—Constance?

—He's Iris's lover, or he was.

—So what was that about?

—I do have a life, you know.

—Why do you need to know when he finishes?

143

—She's trying to get him back.

This made no sense.

—She never mentioned it to me, I said.

She went to the window. She picked up a book and opened it. Then she closed it and put it on the table. She may have been poised but she was nervous as a trapped bird. Her lips were moving.

—Constance.

—What is it now?

—Tell me something. Why are you mixed up in your sister's love affair?

—It's what sisters do. If you had one you'd know.

—If I had a sister I'd keep her in line.

—Like you keep me in line.

How to describe the tone here? Facetious. It wasn't serious. She assumed I was worried about her. So my concern was paternal. She thought she was safe.

—Like I keep you in line? I said. As if!

She lifted her shoulders and opened her hands. The gesture was too theatrical. She asked me how it went with Daddy. She suggested we have a drink, but no, I had work to do. She poured herself a scotch and stood at the window as darkness fell and the streetlights came on.

That night I slept in the spare room behind the kitchen. When I went into the bedroom the next morning she was gone. I found a note on her pillow. It said she had to get away from me for a few days. *I don't want to tell you where I've gone. I know you'll understand. Please don't worry about me. Kiss Howard for me.* Then her signature in black ink in that neat editorial hand. No kisses for me, only for Howard. She had to get away from me, and why? Because I'd overheard her talking like a lover to a man called Eddie Castrol who'd broken her sister's heart. Was I to assume she was with him now?

For two days I tried to suppress my suspicions. I tried to sustain the idea that she wanted to be alone to think through what she'd learned from Mildred Knapp. I'd tried to help her. I didn't know what more I could have done, other than ignore Howard's mother, who was dying. I was forced yet again to confront the fact that *I didn't know my wife. I didn't understand her.* I'd never experienced the kind of shock she'd had, and I'd never felt my identity threatened as hers had apparently been threatened. But I'd made a commitment to see it through no matter what it took, and why? I was her husband. If marriage meant anything I had to do this, for here was the crisis and now it was upon us. She'd asked me to respect her need for solitude and I knew I must allow her that.

★

I was driving east on the Old Montauk Highway. There were no other cars on the road and I was traveling fast. It was a cold day in late winter. The ocean was to my right, loud and violent, big breakers in a high fresh wind. White clouds chased across a blue Atlantic sky. My idea was simple. I'd start with the Windward Motel. After that I didn't know what I'd do. I'd gone to Atlantic City again and Howard told me where she was. I had no idea how he knew it but I couldn't be still any longer for I'd seen her in my mind's eye in the arms of another man, this barroom piano player, this Eddie—

—Should I leave her there?

—No, Papa. Go and fetch her.

I drove into the parking lot of the motel and took a few moments to compose myself. I was apprehensive. I got out of the car. I could feel the wind now and it was strong. I went into reception and the little bell tinkled as I closed the door. There were two chairs upholstered in red vinyl. There was peeling green linoleum on the floor. There was a counter, and behind it a board where the room keys were hung on hooks, and on the wall a calendar showing a Caribbean beach with a palm tree and a girl in a bikini. The wind was howling now, and spitting snow. The quiet young man we'd met before, when we were there in the fall, emerged silently through the curtained doorway at the back. He shivered and rubbed his hands together, hearing the wind, and smiled shyly at me. He had an absent manner that made me think he'd been disturbed while writing poetry. He recognized me. He greeted me by name.

—Your wife's with us, Professor, he said.

He turned toward his board. He touched the empty hook of room 6.

—She's here now.

Alone? I didn't ask. I thanked him. It was oddly dreamlike, to find her with such ease. I'd anticipated difficulty but there was none. I walked down the row of modest white clapboard cabins to number 6. I stood a moment at the door before I knocked. I could hear her voice. She opened the door. She was wearing a white sweater and her hair was damp. She was holding a towel. She was in white slacks and tennis shoes. She looked windblown and wholesome and at that moment she was intensely attractive to me. She seemed to be alone and I wanted to take her to bed at once. I recognized again the recent change in her, it was as though a subtle but unmistakable shift into a new phase of her womanhood had occurred. She was surprised.

—How did you find me?

—Can I come in?

—I guess so.

—Who were you talking to?

—Nobody.

The room was a mess. She was never a tidy woman. The bathroom door was open and from it issued warm air that smelled of soap. She told me to sit down so I shifted some underwear from a chair onto the unmade bed as she stood toweling her hair. I could see no evidence that a man was staying with her other than a comb I didn't recognize. Also she was wearing a thin silver ring I'd never seen before. But her guilt was everywhere apparent to me. It was in her every gesture, her every word.

All false.

Was I right?

It couldn't be true.

This was my state of mind. This is the hell of sexual suspicion. This is what they put you through.

—How are you?

She paused in her toweling.

—Why have you come here, Sidney?

—To take you home.

—I'm not ready.

Why had I imagined I'd be greeted with relief? She was irritated I was there. She still mistrusted me. She was cold and distant. I went into the bathroom. The shower curtain was drawn across the tub but there was nobody behind it and there was no window.

—I thought you understood I need time to myself.

—We miss you.

She sat down on the bed and tied up her hair in a loose knot. She leaned forward and with her elbows on her knees briefly buried her head in her hands. She was talking into her fingers. Then she sat up again and turned to me, smiling.

—It's all right, Sidney, she said. I've had a revelation.

—Another revelation.

—I don't know how else to explain it.

—We have time.

Perhaps Montauk did this to people. I remembered how sweet and loving she'd been when we were here with Howard. Now she wanted to explain why she'd left New York. She was sorry if she'd caused me any anxiety—

—Of course you caused me anxiety, there's no *if*—

—Please let me talk.

There was still that curious quality of calm as she moved around that untidy motel room but at the same time she was hard and brittle. It disturbed me. She was very sorry she'd made me anxious but she had to be near the ocean again. Then she was telling me there was some sort of spiritual contagion at work in Ravenswood. She couldn't go there anymore. It was haunted, she said, but not in a good way—

—Oh for Christ's sake!

—Sidney, *will you shut up!* I'm telling you something. You never listen to me.

She stood over me, frowning at me where I sat on the one chair in the room, recently divested of her underwear. There was a kind of fierceness I'd only felt from her when she expressed her hatred of her father. I told her to please go on. I wouldn't interrupt her again.

—It was spur of the moment but it was where I was meant to come. Here, I mean.

I let this pass. I didn't ask her what cosmic agency organized her itinerary. She was meant to come back here to Montauk, to the Windward Motel in Ditch Plains. She said she hadn't seen her father's ghost if that's what I was thinking because that's not how it works.

I was thinking no such thing.

—How does it work, Constance?

—I don't think you'd understand. I know I caused you pain but I learned something important.

—What did you learn?

—There's nothing wrong with me. It's Daddy.

—What's wrong with him?

I don't know why I asked, I knew what she'd say. I felt tired to death. I wished she'd just let him go! And instead think about *me!* She was at the window now. She was looking out across the road to the beach beyond and the angry black Atlantic crashing hugely onto the sand. It occurred to me that the man was out there, Eddie, but he'd been warned off, he'd seen the car, he'd watched me come to her cabin. He was somewhere in the dunes, skulking

about. Dense gray clouds hung low threatening rain. There was a
faint grumble of thunder out at sea. She turned her head and flung
a glance at me, then looked back out the window. That glance was
charged not with scorn but pity. She spoke with her back to me. I
couldn't see her face.

—You still don't believe me.

I felt a surge of impatience. In her tranquil assurance I heard
condescension. It made me angry but I bit down on it. There
would be no cross words, not yet, not until we were home. Quietly
I asked her what it was she wanted me to believe.

—Don't use that tone with me. I'm trying to explain something.

—Then please do so.

Another glance over her shoulder. Reproach and pity this
time.

—I'll tell you what's wrong with Daddy.

Now she turned and stared at me. Her back was against the
window. She was gripping the sill.

—When he murdered Walter it made him sick and I got it. I
can't explain it any better than that.

—What did you get?

—The dead feeling. You've seen it.

I was at the end of my tether. I didn't know what to think
anymore. I had to talk to Iris again. She was the only one who saw
any of this with clarity.

—You want me to leave you here? I said.

She sat down on the bed. She sighed, and shook her head.

—No. I'll come.

—Constance—

—I'll come!

And then a peculiar thing happened. It was as though she were again being addressed by somebody but this time her head came up and her mouth fell open. I asked her who was talking to her. She didn't reply. She remained distracted. Her lips moved. This lasted for more than a minute and I watched with astonishment as she communicated with this unseen being. It had never been so clear before what was happening to her. Then without a glance in my direction she stood up and pulled a suitcase out of the closet and began to throw clothes into it. A boom of thunder, closer now.

—I didn't want it to be like this, I said at last. We'll pretend it hasn't happened. You're not ready.

I thought: I won't try to move her. I'll take a room in the motel and stay with her as long as I have to. I'll watch over her. If she needs more time out here I'm offering it to her. I stood up. She gripped my arms. We stood face to face and the current of feeling that passed between us was in equal parts frustration and impatience and distrust. Nothing apologetic or affectionate from her, she was beyond all that. She was frowning. Her lips were moving again. It was as though we were subject to some implacable code that demanded of us that we behave like this because there was no other choice.

We were silent in the car. I didn't know what to say to her. I felt I'd acted foolishly. I'd hoped she'd be pleased to know she was wanted but there'd been little sign of that. It was my last gesture. I didn't know what else I could offer her.

—How's Howard? she said.

The storm broke as we left Montauk. We missed the worst of it.

—Howard's fine. It was his idea I'd find you here.

—How's his mother?

—No better.

Somewhere in Nassau County she wanted to stop for coffee. We sat in a diner watching the traffic and I saw she was becoming more anxious the closer we got to New York. The posture of lofty condescension was starting to disintegrate. When we were back in the car I told her Iris was having a bad time. Her father was becoming increasingly difficult to manage. I saw her lift an eyebrow a fraction, an expression of disinterest. The old hatred rising again, fresh and dark as ever. I marveled that anyone so much in the wrong as she was could behave like an injured party. I wouldn't talk to her about that now. All I wanted was to get her back to New York.

We were slow coming into Manhattan. It had started to snow, large damp flakes. In the dusk, in the glare of the oncoming headlights, as the windshield wipers slapped back and forth, I was eager only for this interminable journey to end.

I parked on the street close to the building and we ran down the sidewalk with our coats over our heads. In the elevator she gazed at me with steady eyes and I heard some faint humor in her voice.

—Back in captivity, she said.

Her reunion with Howard was tender. When I opened the front door the boy ran out of the kitchen into the hallway, where he stood dead still with his shoulders up and his fists clenched and stared at Constance as she entered the apartment. I was behind her with her suitcase. She gave me her wet coat, then sat down on the chair by the low table and pulled off her gloves finger by finger.

—Howard, come here.

He approached her warily. She wasn't smiling. She held out her hands and he took them. She gazed into his solemn face with deep seriousness.

—You discovered my hiding place.

—I guessed it.

—That was very clever of you. Are you some kind of a detective?

—No!

—I think you must be.

—I'm not!

—Then give me a hug.

That was what he wanted. I looked on as they clung to each other. Howard had a way of burying his head in the hollow between her breast and her arm and clutching her tight around the waist. Eventually I'd have to detach him.

After dinner he said good night to each of us in turn. It was an important good night for him. I knew what he wanted to say but I also knew that he couldn't find the words. But his intentions were plain enough. He was profoundly relieved to have her back, for he wanted more than anything that we three be a family again. He knew he wouldn't have Barb for much longer. Constance glanced at me and for the briefest moment we exchanged mutual recognition of his predicament.

Again she reached out her hands to him. When he was standing by her chair she asked him quietly if he was glad she was home.

—Yes I am, he said.

He stared at the floor. He couldn't look at her.

—I don't think you are.

Now his eyes came up, hot with injury and outrage.

—Constance, I am!

She folded him in her arms and stroked his head, laughing a little and telling him that yes, she knew he was. Then she let him go. He stopped at the kitchen door and took a last look at us, I guess just to confirm that it wasn't all a dream.

—Such a great kid, she murmured a little later. She was smoking a cigarette as we finished our coffee.

—I'll clear up in here, I said.

—I'm going to bed. Are you coming?

The question hung in the air for what seemed a small eternity. It hadn't occurred to me that she'd suggest it.

—Yes of course.

—Why the hesitation?

—I'm surprised.

—Did you sleep with Iris?

—No.

She leaned forward and peered at me, smiling.

—I'd understand if you did.

—I didn't.

I held her eye. I was level, steady, serious. I thought: She couldn't know for sure. But she'd seen me hesitate and she trusted her intuition.

—You both had good reason.

—We didn't, Constance. Don't judge the rest of us by your own—

—My own what? I don't care where you sleep.

She was in a rage now. She stood up and went to the door. She turned and said: *Or who with.*

That was it. Something snapped. I couldn't let it go now. We would have to have it out. We had so much work to do, she and I.

The next morning she went back to Cooper Wilder. I knew I'd been a fool to go to Montauk. I said this to Ed Kaplan when I saw him for lunch. He disagreed. He said she'd gone to Montauk for one reason only, because she wanted me to come after her. If she'd wanted to hide she'd have gone someplace else.

Why did she go there if she thought I'd come and get her?

Because the game wasn't over.

What game?

You hadn't suffered enough. You had to be punished for loving her. When you'd paid in full for that she'd stop mistreating you.

You think she was conscious of any of this?

I doubt it.

This conversation I conducted not with Ed Kaplan but myself.

The next day she came in around five. I followed her into the sitting room and closed the door. I asked her how her day had been.

—Fine.

—You want to talk about it?

—I don't think so.

Once we'd talked about everything, or she had. She told me I was more selective, that I concealed things from her. She said that was how spontaneity went out the back door while suspicion came in the front.

—You're nervous.

She turned from the window. Why this intrusiveness suddenly? She felt alarmed, I saw it.

—You know the problems I'm having. Maybe you don't.

—I think you better tell me.

The question seemed to hang in the air like a gas. She went on the offensive.

—Why are you looking at me like that?

—You're having an affair.

I couldn't pretend it wasn't so, not any longer, not after what she'd said the night before.

—No, Sidney, I'm not. That's the last thing I need right now.

—So he finished it? Or did you?

—Don't do this again. I'm sick of you doing this.

She left the room at once and I followed her. She took her coat and walked out of the apartment. I followed her. We descended in the elevator in silence. I gazed at her steadily and she stared at the numbers in the illuminated panel above the elevator doors. She left the building and walked east along the block in the direction of Central Park. I followed her.

Still in silence we entered the park. It wasn't a safe thing to do, this time of the day. Any time of the day. It was March and snow still lay drifted on the balustrades and stonework. The high build-ings on the East Side stood stark in outline against the late-afternoon sky. She refused to answer my questions. She demanded to know why I was harassing her like this. We walked beside the lake. It was still frozen. A cold breeze came up. We saw nobody and it felt sinister to me, the emptiness. The ice on the lake was pocked and striated with here and there animal prints, dead sticks and leaves, small heaps of earth: Nature's detritus that in another season would have sunk to the bottom. But all the muck was on the surface now, exposed in plain view.

I saw the sun, a pale, diffuse orb of light low in the sky over Central Park South. I saw moving figures in the distance but I heard only the faintest roar of the city beyond. Here by the ice it was still. But the afternoon was far advanced and the light was fading fast. Dead leaves began to rustle and shift in the wind. At last she turned to face me. She was angry. Again she demanded to know why I was behaving like this. I made an impatient gesture as though to brush away her protestations like so much chaff.

—It doesn't matter how I know and it doesn't matter how I feel, what matters is that it stops.

—What are you talking about?

I became impatient. She was treating me like a fool.

—It's no good, what you're doing. It'll hurt Howard and I won't allow you to do that. I'm protecting my son.

—I'm not Howard's mother.

—You will be. His mother's dying.

I was as angry as she'd ever seen me but I kept it in check so I could make her understand what I wanted. I hadn't told her that Barb was dying, nor had I consulted her on being her replacement. But I'd heard her talking to a man on the phone. The daylight was nearly gone now. We weren't supposed to be there, it was asking for trouble, it was way too dangerous. She sank onto a bench. Her hair was coming loose and spilling about her face. She looked older, there was a kind of fullness to her now, she seemed sexually replete. I couldn't bear to think there was another man. It made me crazy. She lit a cigarette. A chill, damp mist was rising from the ice. Nobody about, we were alone. She later told me she thought I might murder her there. She said she didn't care so long as it didn't hurt.

—What time is it? she said.

—Six.

—I want to go back.

—Constance, don't ever see him again, do you understand me? If you do I'll divorce you and you won't see Howard anymore.

She didn't want to think about that.

—It's he who decides when I see him, she said quietly.

—What are you saying? I shouted.

She seemed to wake up. What was going on? She laughed a little.

—You heard me talking to Eddie on the phone, she said. You jumped to conclusions.

—I knew already.

She didn't know how I'd found out. I hadn't, of course. She wondered if Iris had told me. Did Iris know? Was it possible? Wasn't there *anyone* she could trust? This was her thought, I saw her thinking it. She rose from the bench and at once felt dizzy. She reached out and I held her. She wasn't thinking straight anymore.

—You shouldn't smoke, I said. I wish you'd tell me how I've failed you.

—Don't start that again. What happens this time?

—We go on.

We walked back across the park, our hands in our pockets and our collars turned up, side by side and a thousand miles apart. I think she was impressed with me. There was none of the eagerness for the lurid details of the thing that men are supposed to display on discovering they've been betrayed. It came later. Did she remember what I'd said to her in London an eternity ago, when I decided we were going to be married: *I'm a fascinating thinker and I love you. What's not to love back?* I was fascinating then, it was true. When did I stop being fascinating to her? Was it my fault? Or had she failed to sustain a willingness to be fascinated? I feared at that moment she might be lost to me. She seemed not to have whatever it is that guides us across deserts, the pole star. She had no moral pole star. It was a function of her mother's promiscuity and her father's neglect. I also realized she wanted this crisis. She wasn't aware of it yet, but she wanted it all to fall apart. That was also her mother's fault. The responsibility of marriage was too much for either of them. I would have to carry it for both of us.

She allowed me to take her home. Later, when Howard was in bed, she sat at the kitchen table exhausted. I'd been calm and sensible in the park earlier, I hadn't raged at her as another man would have done. I knew she was frail. She liked me for that. She was weak and I was wise. I understood why she'd done it. She felt as if she was drowning and had clung to the first warm body that came her way. But it should have been mine.

—Sidney.

I was clearing the table.

—I'm sorry, she said. If that helps.

I nodded my head. It was the best she could do. She was think-ing about what I'd said earlier: *We go on.*

—Are we all right now? she said.

I was astonished. I sat down. I put my hands on the table and stared at her.

—Do you know what you've done? I said at last.

—What?

—You've smashed it to bits. It's gone, Constance. You've destroyed it.

—What have I destroyed?

—Whatever you want to call it. Our covenant. Didn't you realize there'd be consequences?

—I haven't destroyed anything! Can't we go on as we were?

She heard the desperation in her voice and wondered if it helped her cause or hurt it. I saw her thinking this. I could read her thoughts. I remained clinical.

—Then no, we can't go on, not as we were before. I'll say it again, there are consequences. I don't want to talk to you right now. I'm going out.

—Oh please don't leave me—

I was very angry. I untied my apron and threw it on a chair and left the kitchen, then I left the apartment. I hadn't finished clearing the table but I had to talk to someone.

She told me later she lay in the silent darkness unable to sleep. She said she tried to control the anxiety rising in waves and flood-ing her, and felt as though she were flattened and gasping on some shoreline with her mouth full of weeds and salt. There were scraps and fragments of content involving scenarios of abandonment, but the real force of it was an overwhelming visceral sensation of loss and despair and *aloneness*. Of course she felt alone, I told her, she'd driven away the one person in the world who only wanted to help her. When I got home sometime after eleven I didn't go to the bedroom. She waited for me, then she couldn't wait any longer. She came looking for me. Howard's door was open a crack and the night-light glowed inside. From force of habit she looked in on him and he was asleep. At times it stabbed her to the heart to see this child safe and warm because we kept him so. He was about to lose his mother. The light was on in my study. The door was closed. She tapped at it.

—Come in, Constance.

I was stretched out on my daybed, fully clothed, one hand behind my head, spectacles sliding down my nose, my other hand flat on the incomplete manuscript of *The Conservative Heart* that was lying on my chest. She thought I loved it more than I loved her. What she didn't know was that I'd started to hate it. But I couldn't leave it alone. I couldn't finish it but I couldn't abandon it either. It was like my marriage, that damn book.

—Am I disturbing you?

When had she ever asked me that before? When had she knocked on my door? Before, when she wanted to talk to me she just marched right in.

—Sit down. What is it?

—Are you going to throw me out?

She sat on the edge of the armchair. Her robe fell open. I saw her long bare legs, a faint tracery of blue veins visible under the pale flesh of her thigh. In that moment I desired her. She was unfamiliar to me and despite everything she fascinated me. She covered herself. She felt desperate, she said. I told her Howard needed a mother.

—Iris needed a mother once, she said.

—I'm talking about Howard.

—You've never spoken to me about this before, she said.

—You like the boy. He seems to like you. Where else can he go?

I gazed at her over my spectacles.

—That's it? she said.

—What else do you want to know?

—Where are you going to sleep?

—In the spare room.

—How clipped and tidy it all is, she said.

I desired her, yes, but I wanted to sleep in the spare room. She wasn't ready to fight me then and I was glad of it. I'd had enough of her. I wanted her to leave me alone. She stood up and examined the papers on my desk. She saw a mock-up of a book cover I'd been idly sketching, *The Conservative Heart* in block capitals, my name in smaller letters beneath, all superimposed on a drawing of an eagle perched on a crag. There was lightning in the sky and copious black storm clouds rolling in.

—You knew it would turn out this way, she said. You've always known it.

—What way did it turn out?

—You knew you'd find yourself married to a slut. It's what you wanted.

—I haven't got anything else to say to you.

—I'm serious, she said. You adored me once. Then you realized I was damaged goods and you despise me for it just like Daddy.

—In which case the answer's no, I didn't think I'd find myself married to a slut.

—You thought I was a good woman.

—Yes, Constance, I did, and I still do.

It cost me something to say this but she pretended not to hear it. Instead she stood up and stretched. Now she felt feline: I knew that mood. Cats are flighty, amoral. Promiscuous.

—That's something, she said. I'm going to bed.

She paused by the desk and picked up my sketch.

—What's the opposite of a conservative heart? she said.

What a strange question. I thought about it.

—A fatherless child.

That stung her, as it was supposed to. The fatherless child is the radical, the revolutionary: the one who tears down the institutions that conservatism reveres. For Constance of course it meant something quite different. She left the room, and as she closed the door behind her she said: You should have put a fucking vulture.

★

Constance was in a state of moral collapse at this time. Her father had wreaked havoc with her fragile identity and in her distress she'd run not to me but to a stranger. In the account she later gave me of those days, certain words recur. *Release. Escape. Defended. Trap. Facade. Terror.* When she thought about her life and the problems she faced both upstate and in Manhattan, she believed it was all connected to her childhood. To be confronted with evidence of betrayal from an early age, and to then reflect on the breakdown of her marriage, this was to recognize *determinism* at work, she said. I have little time for determinists. I saw her behavior as another of her increasingly desperate attempts to displace responsibility for what she was doing, and what she was doing was punishing her father by punishing me. I was aware that in Constance's mind I represented a patriarchal principle she felt she must attack. This didn't change even after Iris died, when everything else did change.

For two days after our conversation in Central Park I said nothing. Then one afternoon I asked her to join me in the sitting room. She came quietly enough. She asked me if I had any cigarettes. I didn't. She walked to the window and stared out, drumming her fingers on the sill. She flung herself into an armchair and crossed her legs. She picked at the hem of her dress. I waited a few seconds until the tiny telltale flecks of red began to appear along her cheekbones. Then I asked her to tell me about it.

—What do you want me to tell you?

—The truth.

—The truth! What truth?

I wanted the truth but without having to force it out of her. I think now that I was wrong to do this, because she then told me she'd give me any truth I wanted. I said no, I wanted *the* truth and she said, Fine. She gazed at the ceiling. Her lips moved silently as they had in the motel in Montauk. She then described how this man Eddie Castrol came to her office one afternoon, this was after she returned from Ravenswood the last time. She said she left the building with him and they took a cab to the Dunmore Hotel. I said she must have known him well for him to come to her office like that but she denied it. She then described pacing around his room as he lay on the bed. I asked her when she'd first met him. Why hadn't she said anything about him?

—You were away.

—But when I returned.

—It didn't seem important.

The first time was when Iris took her to the hotel. Constance thought they were just going for a drink but when they went through to the cocktail lounge Eddie was there. He was playing the piano. Iris told her that he was her lover and that this time it was the real thing. Then as they stood in the doorway, watching him, Iris asked her if he reminded her of Daddy.

—And did he? I said.

—No. It was all in her mind.

There'd been some conversation in the cocktail lounge and then the three of them went to a bar in the Village to hear jazz. They'd made a night of it. She smiled a little at the memory of it. Three swells on a bender, she said, but I had no time for that sort of talk. I asked her how the night ended.

—Iris got drunk, Eddie kissed her good night, and I took her home in a cab.

—Who was he looking at?

—What?

—Who was he looking at while he was kissing Iris?

I needed to know this. Constance regarded me as though I were mad. Then she realized what I was after.

—Who do you think?

—Was he looking at you?

—Yes, Sidney, he was. He was looking straight at me.

There was disdain in her tone now. I pressed on. I made her tell me about their next encounter. She'd met him by chance in the subway. They'd gone to a coffee shop near Union Square. What did they talk about?

—We talked about him and Iris.

—What did he say?

—He said it was hard on Iris. She was just a kid. She took everything too seriously.

—What else did he say?

—He asked me if I was faithful.

I'd thought this would be difficult for her. I was discovering it was far more difficult for me.

—What did he say exactly?

—He said: You faithful?

—What did you say?

—Mind your own business.

—You mean you said that to him.

—No. Yes.

They'd agreed to meet in the coffee shop the next day for lunch. She didn't show up. She didn't feel strong enough, she said. I asked her to please continue. Now a few months had passed and they were in his room in the hotel. What happened next?

She told him she couldn't do it.

So why was she there?

—Just come lie beside me, he said.

She lay beside him for a little while but she was very uneasy, she said. He leaned across her to crush out his cigarette in the ashtray. As he hung over her she touched his face.

—You think I'm a fool, she said.

—No, I don't think that.

Again she fell silent.

—Go on, Constance, I said.

He tried to kiss her but she turned her head aside. But she didn't get up off the bed. He still hung over her, his face a few inches from hers. She smelled liquor and tobacco on his breath.

—Then what? I said.

She stared at me and her face was for a moment full of pity. She said she asked him to say something. He said her name. He kissed her.

—Who are you, Eddie? she said.

But it was only the mind giving up the ghost, she said, the last convulsion before it died and anything resembling thinking simply ceased to be. Whatever takes over, she said, it took over. This was why she was there. She wanted to *stop thinking*. She wanted to *stop feeling*. What followed was angry and passive at the same time, she said, and she wept throughout. Later, exhausted, but feeling empty at last, all rage discharged, she lay beside him in silence. She said she'd never known it like that before. She'd only known it with me.

She gazed at me with a pleasant expression, as though to say: So there's nothing to worry about.

—Go on.

—Are you sure?

She then said she understood the immensity of what she was telling me. She doubted that any man could take it.

—Not even you, Sidney.

She laughed, then she said that I'd never be able to forgive her. But hadn't she given me what I wanted? Her tone was casual. She was lighting a cigarette.

—Go on, damn you, I cried.

But when he became aroused again she panicked. She pulled clear of him and sat up with one arm thrust out, palm open and fingers spread, and told him no, it was enough, but he didn't hear her! He turned her on her front and held her down—

A long silence here.

—And then?

—He put it in me.

—Where?

—In my ass.

I felt sick. Constance blew smoke at the ceiling.

—All right, I said, that's enough.

It was more than enough. I'd asked for the truth, was that it? Or was that a story she'd just invented so as to cause me pain? If that's what she intended she'd succeeded. I tried once more. I was nothing if not a glutton. I asked her how often.

—How often? she said.

—Yes, how often!

She told me they'd had sex seventeen times altogether and each time she wept, she didn't know why.

—Did he give you that ring? I said.

—Mind your own business.

So much for candor. Of course he did. Who else would have given it to her?

Was it only the sex?

Eddie Castrol wasn't the type of man ever to speak of his feelings, but he seemed to want her and it was enough.

So it was only the sex, and the sex occurred because she was in shock after discovering what had happened to the man she believed to be her father.

Afterward he'd go back downstairs to the cocktail lounge. She'd follow him a few minutes later. She'd watch him from a dark booth as he played songs of loss and heartbreak.

I told her I had one last question.

—Shoot, she said with placid composure.

—What about Iris?

—What about her?

—Does she know?

—She doesn't know unless you told her.

—I haven't told her.

EIGHT

I WAS IN Iris's apartment in Chinatown. The Bowery seemed more depressing every time I went to visit her. I felt dread there, a sense of imminent violence. The voices in the street were angry. The gestures were threatening. A woman alone down there wasn't safe. I told Sidney that Iris should move uptown, at least to the Village. Better to be among bohemians than psychopaths. One day I had to step over a dirty bum lying asleep in the lobby of her tenement and it was so dark I almost trod on his head. I tried to give Iris money but she wouldn't take it. Too proud. Too stubborn. Stupid girl, I thought. She needed a man in her life but ever since it ended with Eddie there'd been a few one-night stands, nothing more, she said. She didn't confide in me anymore. I suspected she knew I'd had a hand in the breakup.

It was five in the afternoon and I'd come down on the subway after work. Her door was open when I got upstairs and she was in her bathrobe still. Her hair was tied up in a messy knot and she was wearing her black-framed spectacles. She'd gained weight. She looked older. She'd lost that buoyant, girlish bloom. I must have said something because she started to tell me about her new plan. She was spending the last of her savings on a six-week course in bartending. Through some operation of her own bizarre logic she thought that if she worked around alcohol she'd drink less of it. I told her she was insane. She said maybe I was right. Then she asked me how it was going with Sidney. I didn't tell her he was about to throw me out on the street for what I did with Eddie Castrol. Instead I said he was worried about his book. He couldn't finish it. She listened with lowered eyes. I'd never seen her so cast down and I was disturbed. Iris didn't bottle up her feelings. Then she told me about a rumor she'd heard.

—They're closing the Dunmore.

—Eddie's out of a job then.

I thought, Say the man's name or you'll make her suspicious.

—Don't you care? she said quietly. I've seen you there, you know.

I asked her what she was talking about. More than once, she said. Then I had my head in my hands. For weeks she'd been going to the hotel just to watch him pass through the lobby. She often talked to him, she liked to make her presence known. She'd seen me go upstairs with him and again in the lobby on my way out.

—Got a cigarette?

She flung a pack on the table. I asked her if she'd talked to him about me and she said, Oh yes. Eddie hadn't told me any of this. She went over to the window and looked down at the street for a while.

—How could you do that to me?

—I know.

—You had no *right* to do that! Not without asking.

—I know.

—You're supposed to be on my side.

I heard her resentment but no real rage yet. Then she sat down and started to cry. She turned her head aside and tried to stifle her tears. Her hair was coming loose and falling over her face. My forehead was clamped in my palm and I was smoking. I wished she'd just scream at me and be done with it, this was like the Chinese water torture, drip drip drip. I could have mentioned what *she'd* done to *me*, that for years she'd known who my father was and never told me. But none of it seemed to matter anymore.

—I won't survive this, she said. She stared at the floor, shaking her head.

Oh, enough!

—Okay, I'm sorry!

—Don't you get mad at me, Constance, you're the one who screwed up here!

I rose to my feet. I opened my arms. Again she turned her head away. I told her that if it was any consolation he'd fired me too. It was over. Sidney found out. There was a long silence. Then she spoke.

—He did the same to me, she said quietly.

The atmosphere shifted and I saw at once what was happening. She was saying Eddie used her too. Used her, then fired her. She wanted him for a scapegoat. She couldn't lose us both. It would be too much to bear. She wanted to see what I'd done in the light of her new understanding of Eddie's character. It was just another piece of his cold black heart. I'd have agreed to anything right then.

—I guess so.

—You didn't stand a chance, she said.

—Nor did you.

—I do now, she said.

—What?

—Constance, she cried, I didn't *want* to tell you I knew! I thought you had enough to deal with. He was through with me, so why shouldn't you have him? I honestly tried not to care. But you should have asked—

We were shoring it up, or Iris was, she was clutching at the first narrative that came to hand that made some sense of the whole sorry mess. It was a brave, desperate, generous impulse and I made no attempt to contradict what I knew to be a skewed version of events. Iris wanted to save me and I wanted to be saved, at least from her misery, so Eddie took the fall. Despite what she still felt for him, despite her conviction that her love obeyed some kind of predestined imperative to grow like a tree, an essential goodness in her nature dictated not that she panic and become hysterical that her own sister, *her own sister*, had jeopardized her very shaky prospects but instead that she show sympathy with that sister and find common cause with her, the woman she'd watched more than once as she emerged from the room—from the *bed!*—of the man she loved.

So it would have to do. We were rebuilding here before the thing had even been demolished. Our position now was that he'd had us both, one right after the other, serial conquests, the Sisters Schuyler. At last she allowed me to embrace her, and we clung to each other. We were more liquid than solid by this time. But I was sufficiently detached to wonder at my good fortune, I mean that having done possibly the worst thing a woman could do to her sister that I'd been so swiftly absolved.

Later we went to a bar and I told her how it happened. She was like Sidney, she had to know. I didn't tell her I went to the Dunmore to hear him play, I told her I'd met him by chance on the subway. It was sort of true. I had met him on the subway but nothing happened. He was as I remembered him, cheerful, sardonic. Droll. He'd caused Iris a lot of pain but I didn't hold that against him: If you're not on the receiving end it's easy, and I sure as hell felt no indignation on her behalf. I didn't say this. We'd had coffee in a diner, I said, and that was also true, then I said we'd had lunch and that was a lie although he did at least ask me to have lunch with him. I didn't show, of course, I was sure it would end badly if I did. But he did make me feel good, that man. When I was with him a sort of muted sexual uproar was distinctly audible, to my ears at least. I didn't say any of this either. Instead I told her that after lunch I'd gone to the hotel with him. He wanted to play me something he'd written.

—Yeah sure, said Iris.

She was taking a savage satisfaction in hearing this account, it was better than having to create it in her own imagination. She'd become drunk quickly and her spirits had lifted, she was finding it funny now, how the Sisters Schuyler had been waylaid by the same black-hearted rogue.

—Okay, don't tell me, she said. He played you a song then suggested you come up to his room and look at his press cuttings.

—Something like that.

In fact I'd asked him to take me up to his room, or the room the hotel allowed him to use. When I saw the bed I'd lost my nerve but I wasn't going to say that to Iris. There was only so much truth I'd allow her.

—So you get to his room and he lies down on the bed and he asks you to lie down beside him.

That's clearly what he'd said to Iris.

—Yes.

—Then he sits up on one elbow, right? And he pushes your hair off your face and tells you what a lovely creature you are—

I nodded. Iris was weeping a little now. She flung back a shot of bourbon, not her first, gave a quick brief shake of the head, and wiped her eyes. Ha, she said, the cunt. We were in the Lower East Side for this conversation, in a basement bar a few steps down from the street, a long low narrow room with a wall of exposed brick. At the far end beer crates were stacked next to a toilet and that's where Iris wanted to sit.

—Auden used to drink here, she said. He undress you?

—Auden?

· —Eddie.

—Yes.

—What a cunt.

—You said it.

That first time we hadn't done anything in his room except some kissing. He'd tried to get a hand up my skirt but I wouldn't let him and when he persisted I scrambled off the bed and told him to just cool it or I was leaving. Be nice, I said. I walked up and down the room for a while without removing so much as a shoe, my heart racing but my step as firm as ever, my back as straight. I thought I was in control of the situation. He lay on the bed and smoked a cigarette, just as Iris described it, but he made no further attempt on me. He seemed unsurprised to find himself with a woman who willingly accompanied him to his hotel room and then wanted only to talk. I told him again that I couldn't do it.

So why was I there?

—Just come lie beside me.

I lay beside him for a while but I wasn't comfortable. He leaned across me to crush out his cigarette in the ashtray. As he hung over me I lifted a hand and touched his face.

—You must think me such a fool.

—No Constance, I don't think that.

He made to kiss me but I turned my head aside. But I didn't get up off the bed. He still hung over me, his face a few inches from mine, his lank, oily hair falling over his forehead. I smelled liquor and tobacco on his breath. Something seemed to break inside me. My breathing was very shallow. I didn't recognize him so close up.

—Say something, I whispered.

I wanted to know it was him. He said my name. He kissed me.

—Who are you, Eddie?

Oh, it was only the mind giving up the ghost, the last convulsion before it went quiet and closed down and anything resembling thinking simply ceased to be. Iris wouldn't understand anything of this. She'd always known what she was there for. Whatever it is that takes over at such times, it took over, that's how it was with Iris. But me, I wanted to stop thinking, yes, and I wanted to stop feeling, but then when I realized how aroused he was I panicked. I pulled clear of him and sat up with one arm thrust out, palm open and fingers spread, and told him no, it was enough, but he didn't hear me. *He didn't hear me!* He turned me on my front and held me down and it was only after I started screaming that he released me and sat back on his knees, and I scrambled up and away from him and fled to the bathroom and locked myself in. I stood with my back to the door for several seconds.

—Hey, babe? Constance?

I said nothing. I straightened myself up. I stared at myself in the mirror.

—Constance, are you okay?

When I emerged I was calm. We were both calm.

—Christ, Eddie, you scared the life out of me.

He sat on the side of the bed, pushing his fingers through his hair as he stared at the floor. Then he lifted his head and grinned at me. He shrugged, as though to say: It's only sex. It wasn't only sex to me, it was a very complicated act of sublimation and that's why I'd been unable to go through with it. I sat down beside him. I put my arm around his shoulder. I pulled him to me.

—Eddie, sweetheart, I murmured, we have to make some rules.

Then I got up off the bed. I collected my purse and my hat and coat and went out of the room and down the stairs. Like a drowning woman I was making a last clutch at sanity. I wanted to get back to my office. I'd stood at the edge of an abyss, I'd even looked in, but all at once I had to get to a place of safety. I sat in a cab in a blank state of numbness. In the elevator of the American Electric Building I examined my face in my compact then ran my hands over my blouse and skirt. I was sure there was a stain visible somewhere on my person. But going through to my office everything seemed reassuringly normal. I caught no glances that then darted away, no half smiles that were quickly suppressed. No hint of a suggestion that it was shatteringly obvious where I'd just been. Later I realized I was the last woman in New York of whom such activity would be suspected.

Iris was rambling and smoking and I sat beside her on a lumpy barstool, nodding from time to time, remembering this fiasco, this pathetic display of pusillanimous sexual timidity.

—So when you were with Eddie, I said, in his room—

She had been growing maudlin with the bourbon, but now she brightened.

—Yeah?

—Who fucked who?

She gave a shout of ribald glee. She slapped the counter.

—Me!

I'd gone back the next afternoon determined not to be timid and I wasn't. What followed was angry and passive at the same time, and I wept throughout. Later, exhausted, but feeling clean at last, all rage discharged, I lay beside him in silence. I'd never known it like this. I'd only known it with Sidney.

That afternoon I'd stayed at my desk later than usual as though to convince my colleagues, who in reality suspected nothing, that I was exactly what they thought me, a fastidious and virtuous woman. I arrived home to find Sidney in the sitting room with Ed Kaplan.

—Come and join us, he said, we're just talking faculty politics.

—We'd prefer to hear publishing gossip, said Ed. We've heard about your moral turpitude.

I was standing in the doorway removing my hat.

—We're all as pure as the driven snow, I said.

Later Sidney asked me if I was okay. He said I'd seemed upset. What could he do?

—There's nothing you can do.

I was a little disgusted with myself. I put it down to emotional exhaustion. I'd never have gone back to the hotel if I hadn't been so angry. I was oddly restless, I remember, and drinking more than usual, but after a few days, after a few gins, I found I was no longer repressing, instead I was starting to *indulge* the memory of that second afternoon in Eddie's hotel room, and without feeling any revulsion or shame. It excited me now. I found myself pacing around the apartment like some feline creature and I felt dangerous. I knew what was happening. While I was with Eddie I forgot Daddy, I forgot Sidney, I forgot my anger, and my grief, I even forgot my poor sister; instead I felt careless, clean, *released* in a way. It was disloyal, of course, worse than disloyal, but did Sidney care, if he knew nothing about it? Was he hurt by it? Did it matter, in the scheme of things? It could have ended after I left the hotel that second afternoon, and probably it should have done, but being suspected of nothing I realized that if I wanted more I could have it.

So I went back. This time I was clear about what I wanted. I stood in the doorway of the cocktail lounge. Without hesitation

Eddie stood up from the piano and took me upstairs. There was no panic now.

After that the thing developed fast. The next day he waited for me in the street when I left work. I walked right by him and he followed me. We had sex five times in all, and every time I wept. I couldn't tell him why. But I found I could edit manuscripts and think about him, and I could attend meetings with my mind focused on the business at hand, and at the same time sustain a quiet fever of anticipation at the prospect of our next encounter. At home I was attentive to Howard and Sidney both, and Sidney was gratified by the attention I paid his son. But on the few occasions I was able to slip away from the apartment, or from my office, I went to the Dunmore Hotel, or I joined him in a bar on the West Side where we wouldn't be recognized. He knew a doorway in an alley nearby where I opened my coat for him.

After a time I thought I might be falling in love. It alarmed me a little but later I decided I didn't care. I wouldn't fight it. With something like clinical dispassion I watched the symptoms develop. I suspected Eddie Castrol was the only man I *could* love then. I concealed my feelings from the world, from Sidney, I mean, and the people I worked with, and Iris, until I discovered she'd known all along. The old icy hauteur, the poise and confidence I'd always projected, this was the mask I employed.

One rule I'd made was that he must never call me at the apartment, and I mustn't call him from there. But late one afternoon, this was about ten days after the affair first began, I couldn't help myself. I stood in front of the big bay window that overlooked the street. It was dusk. I was alone. I was troubled by a conversation we'd had the night before. We'd been talking about Iris. I told him I had just one question to ask him and then I'd never mention it again. I asked him if he still loved her, and he said, Who?

—You know who.

—She's right here in the bed. You want to talk to her?

I told him not to torture me. Then I asked him when he finished tonight. But abruptly I rang off. Somebody had come into the room. Sidney was sitting in an armchair, watching me.

—I didn't hear you come in, I said.

—That was Eddie?

I walked to the table. How much had he overheard? I replayed the conversation in my head. I heard myself saying: *Don't torture me.*

—Constance.

—He's Iris's boyfriend, or he was.

—I know who he is. So what was that all about?

—I have a life of my own, you know.

—I'm curious. Why do you need to know when he finishes?

—He's trying to get her back. He wants my help.

—This is the man who broke her heart.

—So she says.

He sat frowning. He was thinking it through. I stood at the window. I picked up a book on the sill and opened it. Then I closed it and put it on the table.

—Constance.

—What is it now?

—Tell me something. Why are you mixed up in your sister's love affair?

—It's what sisters do. If you had one you'd know.

—If I had a sister like Iris I'd keep her in line.

—Like you keep me in line.

How to describe the tone here? It wasn't serious. He was still worried about me. He understood I wasn't strong. His concern was paternal. I was his wife. I was safe.

—Like I keep you in line? he said. As if!

I lifted my shoulders and opened my hands. I suggested we have a drink, but no, he had work to do. He went off to his study. I poured myself a scotch and stood at the window as darkness fell and the streetlamps came on. He so easily could have guessed the truth. But I decided he'd heard nothing to arouse his suspicion. He never intruded on my private life, and anyway his own life was of intense interest to him at this time. He thought he'd found a way to make a coherent book out of the mess *The Conservative Heart* had turned into.

I went to the hotel the following afternoon. I told Eddie what had happened. Sidney worried him. Sidney was smart, he said. He asked me what he'd heard of our conversation and I tried to reassure him. But I managed instead to arouse my own anxiety. I was suddenly filled with a profound unease.

NINE

CONSTANCE ALMOST DESTROYED our marriage for the sake of this affair but she'd never speak about it again. It was too damaging to her self-esteem, what little of it remained. Of course, she knew nothing about love. She knew something about pain, however, and she was soon to know more. A week had passed since that last difficult conversation and at times I was convinced she'd invented the whole thing, and that rather than punish me by having an affair she'd punish me by making me *think* she'd had an affair. And do it in such a way that I suspected it wasn't true but couldn't be sure of it. This is the hell of sexual suspicion. It wasn't the first time.

I watched her talking quietly to Howard at the kitchen table. He'd started to teach her to play chess. They seemed oblivious to the darkly brooding figure who paced frowning about the apartment attempting to spread gloom and menace, but failing: no Heathcliff I. It occurred to me that in this time of radical uncertainty I could believe whatever I chose to, and for some minutes I entertained the idea. But that way madness lay. I decided instead to attempt to accept uncertainty, yes, but only until the truth was revealed. This didn't trouble me because I knew the world to be constructed of stronger material than that, I mean the flimsy stuff peddled by the relativists, a shabby bunch more disreputable even than the determinists. No, there were a number of ideas about which I could be certain.

Name three.

Free will. Death.

★

The call came about five in the afternoon. I heard the telephone as I was leaving my study. I couldn't know, when the phone first started ringing, that forever after there'd be a cleft in time: what came before, what came after. It was Mildred. She asked me if I was alone. I thought, it's the old man. It's Morgan. I listened in silence. I told her we'd drive up to the house tomorrow. I hung up. I found Constance and Howard at the kitchen table, both staring intently at the chessboard as Howard removed Constance's queen with a pawn.

—Check.

—Howard.

—Can it wait? said Constance.

—No.

I took Howard into the hall and closed the kitchen door. I was finding it hard not to cry. Quietly I told him what I'd just heard from Mildred. His eyes grew wide. This was going to be very difficult for Constance, I said, did he understand that? He nodded his head. I told him please to go into the kitchen and ask her to come to my study.

When she came in I asked her to sit down. She was frowning. Then I gave her the bad news. At once she rose to her feet and spread her hands across her mouth. She stared at me for several seconds. Then she began to push her fingers through her hair. She turned away from me and went to the window. She turned back.

—Drowned? she whispered.

She doesn't have the equipment to deal with it, I thought.

—Oh no. Oh dear god.

I waited for the grief to burst through. It was a long time coming.

—*Drowned?* she whispered again. *Where?*

She sank onto the daybed.

—Who called, Mildred?

I sat at my desk and watched her. She was in a state of shock. I knew what it looked like now. I'd seen it after Morgan told her he wasn't her father.

—How did it happen?

—It wasn't an accident, I said.

—What are you saying?

With wild streaming eyes she stared at me. It hadn't occurred to her that she was responsible.

—I told Mildred we'd go up tomorrow.

—Yes. It's too late now.

Shocked, distracted, stupefied almost, she wandered out of the study. I didn't know how long it would take her to assimilate this news.

It was raining in the morning. We left around ten. She'd taken a pill when she went to bed and she was still half asleep. I'd called Mildred and said we were both coming. She said she hadn't yet told the doctor and asked me could it wait until we got there. I said that would be the best thing. I told her I'd look after the formalities. Constance heard me and said there were times it was good to have an adult around.

We were slow getting out of the city because of the rain. It got easier on the Taconic. She began to wake up.

—What did you mean, it wasn't an accident? she said.

—Don't you know how unhappy she was?

—What woman isn't? We don't go drown ourselves.

I glanced at her. She was staring straight ahead. She didn't want the conversation yet. I decided to say nothing more. I put my foot down and the big Jaguar surged past the traffic and soon we had the road to ourselves.

It was a strange uneasy house we came to. The rain had stopped and the sky was clear. Mildred heard the car and came out on the porch. In the cast of her face, in the tight lips and steady eyes, I read sorrow like a ghost beneath the skin. Mildred never embraced others, although Iris used to fling her arms around her, to Mildred's awkward pleasure. Now we performed formal clasps, body to body like distant relatives come together after years apart.

—I haven't told him yet, she said.

—I'll do it now, I said.

—Better later. He wasn't well this morning.

I knew what she meant by that. He was demented.

—Where is she? said Constance.

—Poughkeepsie, at the morgue.

—Sidney, I want to see her.

Mildred said she had the number we should call.

We went into the house. A kick to the heart: hanging off a hook by the door, Iris's denim jacket. Unopened pack of cigarettes in the top pocket. I'll have those, said Constance. Where was her fur coat? She'd gone in the water in it, I thought. It would have dragged her down, no second chances in a coat like that. I left our suitcases at the foot of the stairs and we went along the corridor to the kitchen. Constance sat at the table and lit one of Iris's cigarettes. Mildred had one too. They stared at each other across the table. No trite expression of mutual condolence necessary. Constance reached for Mildred's hands and tears came, yes, even from Mildred. The two women sat silently weeping as the cigarette smoke drifted upward. I went into the sitting room to use the telephone there. The old man was still asleep upstairs.

I went out the back door and walked down through the pines and across the tracks to the river. I'd imagined her standing at the end of the dock in her fur coat, in the darkness, with a bottle in her hand, unsteady, swaying, shouting, weeping, then tipping forward into the chill water, her arms outspread, and in her heavy coat she was lost at once and the river carried her to the haunted pond they knew so well from their childhood—

The dock had largely disintegrated. A section of the planking had given way and the pilings were sticking up out of the water at wayward angles. So she must have been plunged into the river without warning and couldn't claw free of the current. She'd have been carried swiftly away, so no, I was wrong, she didn't give herself to the river, unless of course she'd wrecked the dock herself, to make it look as if—

No. No.

But if she *had* organized it to look like an accident it would have been typical of her, to be so considerate. I stood by the river for some time trying to think it through. What troubled me was this. The man she loves abandons her. He starts an affair with her sister. She discovers the affair. She confronts the sister. She drowns in the river soon after. What is the obvious inference? Unless that wasn't it. But I couldn't believe it. It made no sense. Iris was resilient. She loved life. She had so much to give. She wanted to be a doctor.

Later Mildred told us they'd taken a boat out to look for her.

—Where did they find her?

—Hard Luck Charlie's.

★

We drove to Poughkeepsie. The morgue was on Main Street. Dr. Friedrich met us there. Nothing could have prepared us. We were taken in a metal elevator to a large cold windowless room in the basement with fluorescent lighting and a wall of big steel drawers. It smelled bad down there. Constance at once clapped a handkerchief to her nose. A steel table with drainage gussets stood close to an industrial sink. Iris was naked on a metal gurney. She wasn't swollen or discolored, she hadn't been in the water long enough. She was pale. You'd have thought she was asleep but for the pallor.

We came away in a state of shock and distress. I didn't know if Constance regarded me as her husband anymore, or even if her unhappiness was my responsibility. But I put my arm around her as we walked back to the car. She shook me off. Later, at the house, she sat in the kitchen with a cup of coffee and Iris's cigarettes. Morgan appeared and was surprised to find her there. He asked her why she'd come. Constance called me in from the sitting room and then went out through the back door so I could do what I'd promised to do.

She stood staring down through the darkness to the boathouse and the dock. Time passed with excruciating slowness. What was going on in there? Then she heard what sounded like the sudden cry of an animal in pain. But it wasn't an animal, it was just an old man who'd been told that his child was dead. It was the most painful duty I'd ever had to perform.

In the morning I went back to the city. I needed to get home for Howard. I asked Constance if she was coming with me but she wanted to be near Iris, to commune with her in some manner I didn't even attempt to understand. Her sister was gone but the house and the property were alive still with her presence, she said, and she wanted to breathe that air as long as it carried the faintest trace. She believed that Iris wanted her there. I think she also believed that Iris didn't go in the river by accident. As for the old man, it wasn't hard to be with him because he was broken. He sat in his chair in the kitchen abstracted and silent, uninterested in whatever was put in front of him or said to him. He couldn't be alone for more than a minute or he began to panic. Before I left I talked to Mildred in the sitting room, out of his hearing.

—He'll die if he doesn't eat, she said.

—Mildred, I said, he'll eat. Give him time. It's a shock. He's not strong now.

She nodded. She wanted reassurance.

—You think she did it on purpose?

—No, I said, I do not.

I learned later that Constance went down to the broken dock that night and told Iris she was sorry. It was a clear night and the river was quiet. She gazed out across the water and heard nothing but a distant train. Other than that there was silence. I don't know what else she'd expected. There was nothing out there. Iris wasn't out there. It made no difference to anything, her saying she was sorry.

★

We buried her in the Rhinecliff cemetery next to her mother. The weather was clear and cold. Mildred got the doctor into his dark suit. He'd allowed himself to be led out to the funeral limousine, and a few minutes later into the church, where many more people showed up than we'd expected. Iris had touched a lot of lives, both here and in the city. I brought Howard up for the funeral. When he saw Constance, the boy grew shy. He couldn't look at her. Mildred and Constance stayed close to the doctor and after the service they helped him to the graveside, one on each arm. He barely responded to the mourners who offered him their condolences. It's a travesty of Nature, a father having to bury his child. Constance told me she wasn't given the chance to bury her father, she didn't even know what happened to his ashes. Mildred said they probably went in the river.

We were sitting in the kitchen afterward, exhausted by the events of the day. The old man was asleep upstairs. Constance asked me to come outside. She had something to tell me. She'd decided to stay on and look after him. Someone had to. Mildred couldn't be expected to do it all. So I asked her if she felt she had to make amends, if she had to *atone*. It made her angry. No, she said, she didn't have to atone for anything. Then why? *Someone has to*, she hissed, and I left it at that. I believe she felt she'd driven Iris to it. I wasn't so sure. But whatever the truth of the matter, there was certainly enough she *should have* been guilty about, and I felt no obligation to lighten her load.

I also knew that the one who'd suffer most by her decision was Howard. He'd miss her. He needed a mother. He wasn't an easy boy to love but Constance loved him, and my own feelings for Constance at this time were closely bound up with her relationship to my son. She was closer to him than I was, and she understood him better than I did. Now she wanted to retire to this broken-down house on the river and look after the old man, whom she hated, and Howard would lose the only real mother he had. I felt sorry for the boy but I didn't know what I could do for him. Later I tried to speak to him about it but without success. Like Constance he sustained an inscrutable private inner world. I just hoped to god he didn't hear voices.

After we'd left for the city Mildred moved out of Ravenswood. She'd decided to stay with one of her sisters in Rhinecliff for a while. With Constance in the house she felt she didn't need to be there all the time. She felt it was the tactful thing to do. That night Constance cooked a meal for the old man. He'd come down after

I was extinguished and I welcomed it, I sank into it with relief that I didn't have to sustain a self that was intolerable to me now. One morning after Mildred returned I heard him ask her about the woman who'd been in the house last night. Who was she? Mildred said she was Constance.

—Who's Constance?

—Your daughter.

She didn't know I was in the corridor, listening.

—You mean Iris, he said.

—Yes, Iris.

—She looks after me very well.

We both knew he was clinging to a very few certainties now and that in his mind there was light enough for one daughter only, and she was Iris. I'd find him in Iris's room with no idea how he'd got there or why. Gently I'd lead him back to his own room.

Sidney knew I hated Daddy and he didn't understand why I was doing this. I'd told him someone had to and it was the truth. But it wasn't the whole truth. The whole truth was, I had to get away from *him*. After he found out about Eddie he watched me like a hawk, he asked me questions, he thought about what I said and what I did, always trying to make sense of me, always *dissecting* me. Trying to figure out what I was and failing to see I was nothing. In the early days it had been so much easier. Then he let me be. Not anymore. I needed him but I couldn't take the constant surveillance. I remember one day we were discussing the Wordsworth lines about the murdering intellect. Nothing exceeds knowledge, he said, and I said, Oh yes it does. But he didn't get it. I felt I was locked in perpetual conflict with him. I'd once felt that way about

Daddy but then he'd started having strokes and grew weaker. That's what I needed Sidney to do, grow weaker. But as it stood he wouldn't let this happen and I was exhausted and that's the reason I went back to Ravenswood. I said it was to look after Daddy but I didn't give a damn about Daddy, him I wanted to die. But now I was too much alone with him.

—Constance, said Mildred one day, do you want me to move back into the house?

—Mildred, I said, I do.

I'd hoped she'd ask. It was the first expression of the bond that developed between us over this period. Later she told me it was only when Iris died that she realized I'd been persecuted all my life for no fault of my own. Too little, I thought, too late, but at least someone understands. So she moved back in. She appeared at the front door with her suitcase. I welcomed her as though she were a relative in need of a long vacation. Daddy insisted on taking her suitcase. He went off up the stairs with it. We followed him. He went directly to Iris's room. He set down the suitcase at the end of the bed. There were no sheets on the mattress and I'd already removed the few possessions she'd left there. Some items of clothing and makeup, a doll with no eyes called Amanda Jane.

—You'll be comfortable here, he said.

I'd meanwhile made up Mildred's old bed in the tower.

—This was my daughter's room, he then said to our astonishment. She slept here the night before she died. It was haunted by her presence for a time but she's gone now. You won't be disturbed.

Then with some gravity, his eyes downcast, he left us there. I sat down on the mattress and stared at Mildred. What did it mean? It meant nothing. It was just one of those rare moments when for no apparent reason a stray shaft of light broke through the darkness and briefly gave him a little clarity. Something similar had occurred a few days earlier. It was an afternoon in the early spring when I walked with him through the high grass on the south front of the house to look at the river. There was a cool breeze coming up through the trees. We stood in silence and then he spoke.

—I hope to die soon, he said.

—Don't talk like that.

—It's not a life, what I have. Better off dead.

He fell silent. Sometimes he touched my heart, despite every-thing. An hour later we were having coffee on the verandah.

—Daddy, you remember that thing you said a while ago?

But he didn't remember.

The weather grew warmer and I knew we must make repairs to the house before the next winter. But I had so little money now. I'd taken an indefinite leave from Cooper Wilder and there was nothing coming in. We knew the dementia would kill him in the end but it might not happen for seven years. The house was old and in poor repair. The roof had to be fixed. When it rained it leaked and emptying buckets was at times a daily task. I took on the mowing of the grass near the south front but when the mower broke down I abandoned it and the grass grew high and wild. I sat at the kitchen table and wept. I'd done the right thing to get away from Sidney but I was paying a high price for my freedom. I'd forgotten how dependent on him I'd become during our short marriage. I sold some furniture that had been in the family since colonial times. It didn't fetch much. There was no market for American antiquities then.

But I had some possessions still in New York. There was the Jerome Brook Franklin view of the Hudson in oils Sidney gave me for a wedding present. I wrote asking him to take it to a dealer. Three days later a letter arrived. I at once tore it open. A single folded sheet of paper, and in it a check. He'd been generous. The letter wasn't long. He said that Howard missed me. I'd heard about his mother's death and I'd sent a letter of condolence, a short one. Poor Howard. I knew what it was like for a child to lose his mother. I saw Iris go through it. Later I learned she'd died in the hospital. It was kidney disease. Sidney told me Howard never spoke of her again and never shed a tear, at least not in his presence. This impressed me. Howard knew the proper way to behave. I'd seen Iris grieving for Harriet, and what a piece of theater that was.

Later I thought Howard should have wept. He should have grieved. I hoped to god he wasn't catching my disease.

I thought about Iris at times but not often, because whatever remained of her I'd absorbed into myself. The thing now was to attend to the living. To let the dead be, and attend to the living. I put Sidney's letter away and returned to the kitchen, where I got down on my hands and knees. I was cleaning the oven. It hadn't been done in years. It was like a charcoal pit in there. It was a job that called for scouring powder, buckets of hot water, scrubbing brushes, and what Harriet used to call elbow grease.

A few days later Mildred went upstairs to wake Daddy from his nap and found him sitting in the bathtub. It was a deep old tub with tarnished brass taps and clawed feet. If there was enough hot water in the tank it made for a blissful lingering immersion. Mildred came to the top of the stairs and shouted for me. When I got upstairs she was disinfecting the old man's wrist. He sat in a few inches of tepid water with strings and spools of blood floating around him. The bloody razor lay in a bucket under the sink. It was an inept attempt and he was unsure what had happened. But he grew excited as Mildred worked with brisk efficiency. She murmured to him, comforting him. There were no recriminations. He was skinny and slack-skinned now, white-bearded, and excited by what Mildred was doing, although he must have bandaged a cut a thousand times himself. He had an erection.

—Do we need Hugo Friedrich? I said.

Mildred, on her knees beside the tub, paused.

—I don't think so, do you?

—I don't think so either.

He didn't require stitches. We got him out of the tub and into his pajamas and settled him in bed. Did he want a cup of tea? No. In a few seconds he was asleep.

—It'll be sore when he wakes up, I said.

—He won't know why.

We took the razor downstairs and emptied out all the drugs in his bathroom cabinet. It was a new source of concern. We sat in the kitchen with the back door open.

—Mildred, I said, that day Daddy found Walter and Harriet in the boathouse.

I wanted to let the dead alone but it wasn't easy. Earlier that day I'd been to Tillman's Landing. I often went there by myself to lay flowers on the rails. I was grieving for my father. But I didn't feel his loss as acutely as I once had. Always a ghostly figure in my mind, he was now more insubstantial than ever. I was losing him.

—Yes.

—How did he know they were in there?

Mildred reached for my hand. She was gazing at me with compassion, more than compassion, sorrow. Remorse. She said she'd seen them from the tower. She fell silent. She continued to gaze at me. I remembered the long talk we'd had in the truck in the winter. Was she telling me Daddy didn't see them go into the boathouse, but she did? And she'd betrayed them, she'd told Daddy where they were?

—Did you? I said.

She covered her mouth with her hand. She nodded her head. We sat in silence as I took in this news. I turned to her at one point, I remember, and mouthed the word *Why?* She shook her head. I didn't pursue it. I understood why. The situation had become unbearable to her and she wanted it to just fall apart.

—Shall we have a small one? I said at last.

—I think we deserve it, said Mildred, a small one.

Later I realized it wasn't Walter she wanted to destroy, it was Daddy's frail marriage. But she failed. She didn't move back into the house until Harriet was dead. She told me about the deal they made, Harriet and Daddy. He'd raise me as his own but only if Walter's name was never mentioned in Ravenswood again.

—And was it ever mentioned? I said.

—Not until you found out.

So that was the family secret and I was supposed never to know it. I wouldn't have known it if Daddy hadn't started having little strokes and forgetting what the arrangements were. But in a way I'd always known. I'd known there was a secret and it made me ill. It haunted me all my life. But now the crypt was opened, now I knew the truth. Had it set me free? Was I liberated? Ha. Was I hell.

One day soon after this I was sweeping the hallway downstairs. The front door was propped wide open. I heard a car in the driveway and went out onto the porch. It was Sidney's hearse. The black Jaguar. I stood leaning on my broom as he parked by the barn. I saw him reach across and open the passenger door. Howard stepped down onto the gravel. His arms spread wide, he was clutching a flat square object wrapped in newspaper and tied with string. Carefully, slowly, he walked over to the house and climbed up the steps to the porch. He held out the wrapped object.

—Constance, this is a present from me.

The sun had come out from behind a cloud and with the glare off the windshield I couldn't see Sidney's face. I knew of course the gift was from him. I asked Howard if it was really for me, and he said yes, and I thanked him. Then I peered at the parcel. I lifted it to my ear, and shook it, frowning. I loved to tease that child. His impatience was easy to read. Open it now!

So I opened it. It was my painting, the Jerome Brook Franklin, the Hudson at dawn. I dropped to my knees and put my arms around the boy. It was a thoughtful gesture on Sidney's part. I think he wanted me to believe it was more than that. Howard went back to the car. Sidney got out and we gazed at each other across the driveway. He didn't approach me and I didn't leave the porch but I guess it was an important encounter. Howard was simply happy that he'd seen me. That was enough. That was what mattered. But it wasn't the only thing that mattered. Sidney was coming around. He was weakening. I was encouraged by this. Every time I looked at the Jerome Brook Franklin I felt it again. Not triumphal, no triumphalism yet. But encouraged.

The old man's wrist was healing but our vigilance never slept now. We kept tools and sharp knives under lock and key. Talk of death grew more frequent. I remembered a time when Iris and I had been amused by him saying, on being asked if he'd had a good sleep, that no, he hadn't: He'd woken up. It wasn't funny anymore. At times anxiety overwhelmed him after even a few moments alone. To him it must have felt like blackest night. He was a child. He lived in the present moment and suffered his horror unmediated by reason or experience. Without any insight he might have endured his condition, and unable to reflect on it, never desired an end to it.

But he did desire an end to it. One day he realized that if he couldn't do it then I must.

—Iris, why won't you kill me?

I don't remember my answer. I do remember glimpsing a ghastly ironic symmetry at work here, that the man who killed my father now asked me to kill *him*. I asked Mildred if he'd asked her the same question.

—He asked me what I thought I was saving him for. I didn't know what to tell him. What should I have said?

I said I didn't know what she could have said that wasn't a platitude or some other kind of lie.

—Should I talk to Dr. Friedrich? said Mildred.

—He won't help us.

—No.

We came to dread his moments of lucidity because now he was interested in that single topic alone, his inability to die. We decided simply to refuse to discuss it with him. This infuriated him further.

—You think I haven't done it? I've killed my patients!

His tirades could last for minutes. I'd have to leave the room.

—Iris, come back here! Listen to what I'm telling you!

I'd stand in the hallway and count to sixty.

—What are you yelling about? I'd say when I went back into the room.

—What?

But he'd have forgotten. Darkness had descended until the next time. I told Mildred I couldn't take much more of it.

—You have to, you have no choice. Nor do I, said Mildred.

It was summer but the pleasure I might otherwise have felt in seeing the trees in full leaf and the wild flowers blooming, and the butterflies and the birds, the long warm evenings and the sun sinking behind the mountains as the river caught fire in the last of the day, it was all lost in the shadows of the old man in his fury and despair, when he wasn't adrift in a terrible gloom of unknowing. I didn't hate him now. He was Daddy, yes, but not the Daddy that had done me so much harm. He was unable to harm me anymore. But it was like living with death, for nothing issued from Daddy that was any kind of a manifestation of life. I'd be out at the back of the house pinning bedsheets to the washing line when I heard him.

—Iris! Where are you?

I'd go in to see what he wanted.

—Where have you been? I didn't know where you were!

I'd sit with him, thinking of the basket of damp bedsheets waiting to go on the line before nightfall.

—Are you free? he said one evening.

We were accustomed now to the vagaries of his crumbling mind. Sudden statements or questions like this that might be loaded with meaning or mean nothing at all. It was a question he'd asked before.

—Yes, Daddy, I am, I said. Are you free?

—Don't be so damned stupid.

He thought of the house as a prison and the two of us as his jailers. He no longer got angry about it. It seemed he'd become resigned to his situation.

But as the days passed, a change in the household occurred. The old man's insistence that he must die had aroused in each of us, separately, a question. It wasn't an easy thing for us to talk about. We'd underestimated his determination to end his life. Now we began—independently, until the night the question was finally voiced—to entertain doubt. I brought it up first. I expected Mildred to reject the idea at once. I only spoke of it because it had become a habit of our intimacy to say what was on our minds. I wanted Mildred to tell me that what I was thinking was abominable. But Mildred didn't say that.

—I know, she said. But how?

We sat a long time in silence. The next step in this conversation would have to wait for another night. What mattered was that a possibility had been articulated. We left it alone, not because it shocked or frightened us but because we had to consider it.

We moved around the house thinking thoughts of death. I didn't know if the old man understood what was happening. If before he'd been unfree, a prisoner in his own house, there now hung over him a sentence of death. I could feel it in every room in the house. I felt it in Iris's room most of all, that's where I slept now. It gathered in the corners and hung like a mist beneath the ceiling. The air was thick with it. At times it was suffocating. It was almost impossible to breathe. It had an effect on Daddy. It made him quieter, also more childlike: The old man's fire was at last extinguished. There were times we thought he was consciously preparing himself, but this was illusory. Nothing occurred consciously now. He was empty of thought, although Mildred still didn't believe that.

—He knows what's going to happen. He's at peace now.

—How does he know?

—Can't you feel it?

Sometimes I could. Other times I saw only a demented old man shuffling through the house in his pajamas with his penis hanging out like a piece of old elephant flesh. He hadn't a thought in his head until he realized he was alone. Then he panicked. I sometimes thought our decision was premature but Mildred never wavered. And as if to confirm that she was right and I was wrong, Daddy again asked the question he'd asked so many times before: *When will you let me die?*

We decided to do it late one night at the end of the month. There was no moon. We'd had heavy rainfall earlier in the day. I don't know why we chose that night, perhaps because it was so dark. But we both realized it was time. We had that kind of understanding now. We were the sisters of mercy now. We gave him a watery whiskey with a sleeping pill crumbled into it. We sat in the kitchen for an hour and drank whiskey ourselves, not so watery either. It was all oddly solemn.

The two women ascended the back stairs. The world was very still. When they got to his bedroom Mildred opened the door and allowed Constance to enter first. She was carrying the pillow. The drapes were closed. The room was full of shadows. The glow from the bulb at the end of the corridor was all the light they had. The old man's breathing was slow and heavy. It was punctuated by snorts. Mildred stood by the door as Constance approached the bed. He was sleeping on his back. Spittle glistened in his beard. His mouth was open and his lips were damp.

She put the pillow on the bed. Then she climbed onto the bed. Carefully she straddled him, placing one knee either side of his chest. She turned toward Mildred where she stood in the shadows by the door. Mildred nodded her head. She lifted the pillow—

Then he opened his eyes.

I couldn't do it.

The next day I had to go into Rhinecliff. On my return I was parking the truck by the barn when Mildred came running down the porch steps and across the driveway.

—What is it? What's happened?

—I can't find him!

We went through the house. Every room was empty. Only when we got up into the tower did we see him. From the high window we made out a tall dappled figure in pajama pants moving through the trees far below. He was making for the river. We ran downstairs and out through the back door.

As we scrambled down the hill we heard the Albany train approaching. He was in clear view now, splashing through the sedge, his pajama pants soaked, his long arms and legs pumping. The white head was lifted to the sky and he was shouting. He floundered on, losing his footing and pitching forward, then recovering, moving inexorably toward the shallow bank that ascended to the tracks. He was in bright sunshine now, and beyond him the river glittered like a heaving bed of jewels as the locomotive came on. The old man's pace didn't slow or falter. He wanted only to get to the railroad tracks.

On came the train. It shimmered in the heat. We were moving through the sedge as he clambered up the bank on the far side. We saw him glance over his shoulder. We were screaming at him now and he had to hear us even with the noise of the train but our voices seemed only to quicken his progress toward the tracks. We saw that in the next seconds he and the locomotive would at the same moment arrive at the same place. He didn't waver, he didn't flinch. He didn't know what hit him.

ELEVEN

I HEARD ABOUT Morgan Schuyler's death in the late afternoon and drove up to Ravenswood early the following morning. The front door burst open and Constance ran down the porch steps and flung herself into my arms. For a few seconds she clung to me and I felt through her blouse that her heart was beating very fast. Then she put her lips to my ear and breathed the words, *Thank you*. I remembered her telling me once, a lifetime ago, that she'd only be well again when the old man was dead. We walked across the driveway to the house. Her arm was around my waist and mine around her shoulder. Three months had passed since she'd moved back to Ravenswood and her dream was realized: Daddy was dead.

As soon as we entered the house the shadows descended. How dark it was. The verandahs blocked out much of the daylight and the stained oak paneling absorbed what little else filtered through. Where was Mildred?

We sat in the kitchen. The back door was open and the air was sweet with the scent of fresh-mown grass and trees in blossom. Far below us the Hudson sparkled in the sunlight. The railroad tracks were gleaming. Constance sat facing me, her hands clasped together. I tried to detect in her some sign of shock but there was none. She did, yes, seem to be at peace but I wasn't convinced that the old man's death could have swept away her extensive structure of neurosis so fast, and I watched her carefully. I couldn't tell if she was acting or not and she clearly didn't know either.

—How's Howard? she said.

—He talks about you every day.

She grew more animated.

—Soon he'll have me every day! Sidney, we can start over, can't we? When I woke up this morning I felt as though it was the first day of my life.

—You're not devastated?

—He wanted to die. But now I can live! There's so much I want to do! We'll take Howard to Europe. It'll be educational. We'll go to all the great museums. We'll sit in outdoor cafés and see how other people live.

I felt a distinct whisper of foreboding. I was right. She'd assimi-lated nothing.

—Let's bury your father first, I said.

This intrusion of brute reality failed to deflate her.

—Yes of course, let's bury the dead, but let's celebrate the living too!

Did she seriously imagine I could be drawn into this bizarre mood of exultant affirmation? I'd come to make funeral arrangements. She knew what I was thinking. We'd speak of it in some more sober hour. But she wanted a sign from me now.

—You're relieved it's over, I said.

I took her hands in mine. I had to tell her what I felt, or what I feared.

—It's not just a passing thing, is it? I said. You won't come crashing back to earth and decide you hate me again?

She gazed at me through a glaze of tears. She pressed a fist to her mouth and shook her head. She came around the table and pulled up a chair next to mine. We sat close together and she was smiling as the tears ran down her face. I wanted her to melt the ice in my heart but it couldn't be done in an instant. I was too old for that.

Then Mildred came into the kitchen and everything got dark again. Constance rose from her chair to fill the kettle. I stood up and faced Mildred, who stared at me from haunted, startled eyes. She was dressed all in black. She looked as if she hadn't slept.

—I'm sorry, Mildred.

She nodded. She pushed past me to the sink. If there was coffee to be made then she would make it. Her back was bent now. She'd aged a decade in a night. She was a widow once more. Constance had lost them both, Iris and Daddy, but so had Mildred, and Morgan Schuyler, her true love, the love of her maturity, for whom she'd performed silent service all these years, had died before her eyes. I thought: She won't last long.

Constance was standing in the doorway looking out toward the mountains with her back to us.

—Come out for a moment, she said.

Mildred was washing out the coffee pot. Humped, intent, her eyes hooded, her hands busy, she absorbed no light and gave none out. I stepped through the back door and Constance turned to me and took my face in her hands. With careful tender delicacy she kissed me on the lips. I tasted a flicker of her wet tongue, quick as a viper. How long since she'd done that? If she could sustain it, if she could only make me warm with her kisses again, then I'd soon lose the resentment and mistrust all silted up inside me. I wanted nothing more.

—We must look after her, she said.

Once again arrangements had to be made. I was busy on the telephone for most of the afternoon. I spoke to Hugo Friedrich. I'd antagonized him once but it didn't seem to matter now. He was brusque in his sympathy but he was a practical man. He told me what was going to happen and what I had to do.

That night we all retired early. It had been a long time since Constance and I had shared a bed. I asked her if she'd prefer that I sleep elsewhere.

—Where would you sleep? she said.

There were only two possibilities. Daddy's room was empty but it seemed faintly indecent to suggest it.

—I could sleep in Iris's room, I said.

She was turning down the quilt. I stood on the other side of the bed. My suitcase was by the door. She gazed at me. Suddenly she seemed very frightened and very young, and I glimpsed again the fragility I'd seen when we'd first met and fallen in love. How very long ago it all seemed now.

—I'll sleep here with you, I said.

From opposite sides we entered the bed. We turned aside to switch off our respective bedside lamps. We turned back. We moved toward each other in the darkness. The world was very still, very silent. Such a profound silence, in every sense, whenever I arrived from the city.

—I'm cold, she whispered.

To hold her in my arms, to touch her even through the night-gown, was like an electric shock to my poor dry body, inert these many months. We kissed, and again I tasted her flickering wet tongue. Then there was some urgency to the proceedings and it all got rather turbulent, and I had no opportunity to reflect on what it meant for us, nor did I think much of it when after a very few breathless moments she whispered her strange request, that I call her by her sister's name.

★

Morgan Schuyler was buried next to his wife and daughter later that week. Constance stood at the graveside with a wild rose she'd picked in the garden that morning. Not yet thirty and the only survivor, the last of the line. But I feared the aftermath. I feared that having climbed so fast and so high from the depths in which she'd been sunk there must be a collapse eventually. She'd seen her stepfather die under the wheels of a locomotive. She'd seen his body burst apart like a bag of blood.

The next day we returned to New York. Constance was eager to leave Ravenswood and I took this as a good sign. Already she'd told me that she intended to sell the house but there was no urgency, the old man's will had yet to be read. Mildred quietly told us that she would stay on. I wasn't happy about it. She was a bereaved woman and it was an old house in an isolated location. It seemed a morbid situation and I feared that her grieving would take a morbid turn. Morbidity clung to that place and to that family like dank river fog. Constance brushed my reservations aside.

—Mildred's tough, she said.

She remained dangerously exalted. There was a curious incident at the graveside. After she'd tossed the wild rose onto the coffin she'd turned to me and, seizing my lapel, produced what sounded like a muffled shout of laughter. She buried her face in my shoulder. Her whole body was shaking. I put my arms around her. I don't believe any of the others realized what was happening, but this was no access of strong grief. I was the only one who knew it, but Constance was in the grip of uncontrollable laughter. I put it down to hysterical stress. She was a sick woman. The previous night she'd again asked me to call her Iris.

Our return to the city was delayed by a mechanical malfunction. Coming into Staatsburg, the Jaguar began to lose power. I suspected a blockage in the fuel line. I eventually found a mechanic but it was humiliating to have to drive that big car down Main Street at five miles an hour, as though we were part of a funeral procession.

Howard was happy to welcome Constance home. That night we ate together at the kitchen table and no mention was made of Daddy. But still I anticipated the backlash. I was troubled by her refusal to talk about him, and indeed about Iris.

The backlash never came. She awoke each day in a state of zeal for life. There was a light in her eye from morning to night. She seemed to feel neither fatigue nor anxiety, and for sure not grief, not for Daddy, not for Iris. Her sister's name was only heard at night, in bed, during intimacy. My own theory: She thought I'd married the wrong sister and she was trying to make amends. She was allowing me to make love to Iris so as to atone for what she'd put me through. How wrong she was. But I didn't know how to say this without demeaning her lavish sexual generosity.

Meanwhile she attended to the running of the household as she never had before. Poor Gladys grew sullen as she was put to work clearing out obscure closets, opening windows and airing rooms, throwing stuff away. Eventually even Howard grew weary of her relentless spirited briskness. After ten days of so-called spring cleaning, she went back to work. In the evening she explained to me the ways in which Cooper Wilder must modernize.

—The world's changing and if you don't change with it you die, she said.

I'd begun work on *A Scream in the Night*. The progressive tendency in Constance's thinking didn't chime with my own outlook. The transformation of Manhattan into a so-called modern city was to me a bad joke. New York was breaking down. I catalogued its death throes on a daily basis. People told me that living here was a nightmare. Those who could afford to were moving out. The city in its decline was not only more dangerous and more squalid, it was becoming of all things *mediocre*.

Constance was unaffected by any of this. I stood in the doorway of our building one morning and watched her as she walked up the block to the subway. The sidewalk was strewn with trash where garbage cans had been kicked over in the night. There was broken glass underfoot from the smashed streetlights. The sidewalk was cracked and uneven. There were potholes in it, potholes in the sidewalk. Constance was oblivious. She held her head high, and in her yellow coat, with a small matching page-boy hat perched at a jaunty angle on her piled blonde hair, she looked like royalty as she effortlessly, gracefully strode on, untouched by the filth through which she moved.

As the weeks went by I watched her attempt to sustain the appetite for life she'd discovered in the immediate aftermath of Daddy's death. That her energy issued from an unwholesome place in her psyche was made clear to me one night after we'd been to the theater. I don't remember what we saw, but afterward Constance decided we must have a cocktail. I'd have preferred to go home but instead we went to a bar at Forty-fifth and Eighth. It was called the Flamingo or the Ostrich or some damn thing. It was full of smoke. It was crowded and hot and loud. We found a table and ordered highballs. Constance was eager to have a good time. She was shouting at me but I couldn't hear what she said. Just as the waitress was setting our drinks down a man lurched against our table. There was spillage, and Constance at once stood up and threw what remained of her highball in the man's face. Then she seized him by the lapels.

I thought he was going to hit her. I was on my feet too. More shouting. The man's wife appeared. Now there was screaming. Others became involved. I tried to get Constance out of there. She was cursing the man, cursing his wife, the air was blue with her curses. A waiter tried to calm her down. The man told me to control my daughter.

Some minutes later we were out on the street and Constance was still enraged. I put my arms around her, there on the sidewalk at Forty-fifth and Eighth. The crowd surged past us, bumping into us, swearing at us, while Constance broke down and wept on my shoulder. Grief, I thought. Here it is at last. Then I thought: This is what we've come to. On one of the busiest intersections in Manhattan a woman weeps for her dead and nobody gives a damn. Nobody even notices. I once thought it the mark of an advanced civilization when one's private life could be conducted in public. Not anymore. Now it was just another chance to be humiliated.

—My darling, I whispered as she sobbed into my shoulder.

She lifted her head then and stared at me, tears streaming down her face.

—Call me Iris! she cried.

But the incident revealed what I already suspected: Constance wasn't free of the old man yet, her rage was ample proof of that. I think she realized what had happened, for in the morning her mood was subdued. She couldn't meet my eye. But there were other matters I had to discuss with her. I told her we had to talk through what had happened to us.

—Why?

We were in the sitting room. I did what I could to not antagonize her. I stood by the empty fireplace, leaning against the mantel. She paced the floor, smoking cigarettes.

—For Howard's sake. And for our own.

I was disturbed to see she'd lapsed again into a sort of tic I'd first observed when I brought her home from the motel in Montauk.

While she talked to me she seemed to be listening to another voice, and this other voice caused her to frown and make facial expressions unrelated to the conversation. It was disconcerting, but when I mentioned it she smiled in a knowing way that irritated me acutely. I suppressed my anger however, not wishing to quarrel with her. I told her that without Howard the marriage would have fallen apart long before this. He needed us both, I said. Just as we needed him. She didn't dispute it. I knew she would listen to me if I prefaced my request this way.

—Go on, she said.

I told her I had to make sense of what had happened to us so we could go forward with no lingering doubts, or resentments, or forebodings about the future. Was that an unreasonable request? Wasn't it the least we required as a foundation for a working marriage, even a happy marriage? Or what was the same, a *not unhappy* marriage?

Constance was never good at thinking about marriage in the abstract. She saw no moral dimension in it. For her, marriage was fluid, transient, a provisional arrangement, and if it didn't seem to be working then there wasn't much point, was there?

—Do you want Howard to grow up like you did?

This got her full attention.

—I wouldn't wish that on my worst enemy.

—Then let's create a real home for him.

—We have.

—No, Constance, we haven't.

Again I tried to explain to her that without clarity and candor she and I could never be at peace with one another. She was standing at the window with her back to me. Perhaps I was asking the impossible. This woman hadn't known a minute of clarity or candor her entire life. Without turning around she asked me what I wanted to know.

—Everything.

She was alarmed now.

—Like what?

But when I told her she flew into a rage. She wasn't ready for candor, perhaps she never would be.

—Is that what all this candor crap is about, so you can punish me some more? I thought it was over when Daddy died but it's not, is it, it's never over. Well, I've had enough. I won't be punished anymore!

She ran out of the room. I sat on the chesterfield with my head in my hands. It was I who was being punished. Apparently I hadn't suffered enough yet. All I'd done was ask her if she'd told me the truth about the affair with Eddie Castrol. It tormented me, the possibility she'd allowed him to have anal sex with her. I wanted to hear her say it wasn't so. I suspected that when I called her Iris in bed, in her heart she called me Eddie. Then I heard the sound of breaking glass from the kitchen. I found her throwing plates and wineglasses on the floor. She was weeping. She was barefoot. She was bleeding. I heard Howard's voice. I took him back to his bedroom and told him to go to sleep, there was nothing wrong. Then I returned to the kitchen. Constance was sitting on a chair amid the broken glass and china, still weeping. I would have to wash her feet.

There was no more sex after that. She didn't even want me in the bedroom. I could have insisted, but I hadn't the heart to impose my will on her anymore. I moved into the small spare room behind the kitchen. I accepted then that I couldn't do it on my own. But I couldn't make her see a psychiatrist, I'd tried and failed more than once. I talked to Ed Kaplan. He knew much of Constance's story although I'd told him nothing about the affair. Ed was sardonic and wise. This was what I wanted from him. He told me he was frankly astonished that things weren't worse at home.

—What do you mean by that?

—All she's been through?

We were sitting on a bench in Central Park. It was a pleasant day in July. A heat wave was forecast. Ed had grown a beard. It was to frighten his daughters, he told me. They were running wild. They respected no form of authority. It was a familiar theme. If the beard didn't work he planned to prosecute them.

—What can I do? I said.

He pondered this. He was silent for a time.

—She won't see a shrink?

—No.

—Get her to talk about it. Don't let it fester. But Christ, Sidney! One man under a train is bad enough—

—Tell me about it.

A group of teenagers on the grass nearby was singing folk songs and strumming guitars.

—How are you holding up? he said.

I shook my head.

—So, Ed, make her talk about it, that's your advice?

—She keeps acting out. That thing with the guy in the bar. Then smashing all the plates.

—Not all the plates—

—She represses it, Sidney, it only gets worse.

We sat there nodding in the sunshine. Like a crippled sparrow, a song of peace and love struggled past us in the warm summer air. That's as far as we got, Ed and I, that time: talk good, repression bad. When I arrived home I found Constance at the kitchen table reading a novel and eating sardines from the tin.

—Why aren't you at work? I said.

—I quit.

I didn't believe her. She'd been showing up at Cooper Wilder only sporadically and I knew Ellen Taussig was concerned about her, more than concerned, disappointed. Let down. She didn't jump. She was pushed.

★

The heat wave lay on the city like an incubus made of steam. I looked the word up: a male demon who has sexual intercourse with women in their sleep. If this was how the English mama conceived Constance it would explain a lot. And now she'd quit her job. I asked her why.

—Time to move on.

No commitment. I told her she'd laid the foundations of a good career at Cooper Wilder. But no. No loyalty. No tenacity. She'd have abandoned our marriage if I'd let her. Daddy had at least provided some kind of focus for her flailing emotions. As an institution, the family provides structure for women like Constance. But our own small unit couldn't give her what she needed.

I took on Daddy's role as best I could. I tried to be the source of order in her life. I knew she wouldn't leave me, not while we had Howard, for our one source of stillness and peace, our one opportunity to be *not unhappy*, lay with my son. And her chess game was improving. They played every evening now. It gave me respite from my anxiety. It gave me a micron of hope. I thought that if she could only extend to me the simple trust and affection she felt for my son then we could climb up out of this dark place. I would ask her no more questions about the past. It was time to look forward.

Thinking this, I left my study. They were in the sitting room, at the table, silently staring at the chessboard. I saw total engagement, utter concentration, and I was encouraged. We'll get through this, I thought. I collapsed onto the couch and pressed my fingers hard against my temples. I'd been troubled by headaches lately. My nights were disturbed. I got no sleep in the spare room. There hadn't been any sex since she smashed the crockery and I missed it. I heard a small clicking sound, one chess piece making contact with another as it was removed from the board.

—Check.

It was said so quietly I didn't even know whose voice it was. The city was peaceful. Late sunlight drifted in through the bay window overlooking the street, motes of dust dancing in it like germs. It was still very hot. Gladys had brought flowers that morning, I smelled them now, what were they, tulips, lilies? In a moment I would get up off this chesterfield and identify the flowers and then quietly pour myself a drink. I began to float away. Click. Check. A man is running toward a locomotive—

I awoke with a start. Constance and Howard were standing over me where I lay sprawled on the couch with saliva running down my chin. I struggled up, wiping my face with a handkerchief.

—What happened?

—Constance won, said Howard.

—You were shouting, she said.

—I had a nightmare.

A few mornings later Constance took a call from upstate. I heard her cry out. I came out of my study. She was in the sitting room, by the window. I saw her slam the telephone down, then she swept the chess pieces off the board so they clattered all over the hardwood floor.

—What the hell—? I said.

She turned toward me. Her face was twisted with fury. I barely recognized her.

—The house!

—What about the house?

—He left it to Mildred!

—No.

It was Morgan's will, of course. That was his lawyer calling.

—Yes!

He'd left it all to Mildred, the land, the house, the truck, the boat: everything. I was astonished. But Constance was more than astonished. She was speechless with outrage. I spent an hour with her. At first I failed to grasp the real import of this distressing news, I mean the fact that she didn't care about the property, that wasn't it at all. No, what she'd wanted was to tear Ravenswood down.

She'd been looking forward to it. She'd relished the prospect. But now—

—She's haunting the place, Sidney, she's keeping it alive with his memory. I can't bear it. I wanted to watch it come down. I'd have set fire to it myself if they'd let me. But with that old ghost there'll be no peace for any of us.

Listening to this I suddenly saw not Mildred but Constance as the old ghost. The bitterness was eating away at not just her mind but her face, her body, her chattering lips, the very fiber of her soul. Soon it would all be gone. I saw the day coming.

Her mood grew darker. Her morbid vitality was turned inward now. This news from upstate took us both by surprise. I tried to tell her that it made no difference but I saw how far I'd get with that. It was an insult from beyond the grave, one further reason that her hatred of Daddy would never die. She hadn't told me how warmly she'd anticipated the destruction of Ravenswood.

—Every plank and floorboard, Sidney. Every slate, every stone, every *nail*—

She was obsessed with this one idea. She knew better than to pursue it with me, however, because I didn't share her obsession. I found it extraordinary that the old man's death hadn't been enough for her, and that she had to see his house destroyed as well. I realized it would never end. The pathology was rooted so deep in her psyche, the condition was chronic. Unless she sought treatment it would only grow worse.

I was desperately tired. Then one afternoon I heard her in the kitchen telling Howard that Ravenswood was really her house and that one day she'd get it back. I heard him asking her if she was going to live there. This would worry him, of course. He smelled separation and he didn't like it. I knew what was about to happen, she was about to tell him that no, she didn't want to live in it, she wanted to burn it to the ground. He wouldn't understand, of course, and I didn't want him trying to understand. I stood in the doorway.

—That's enough, I said quietly.

Howard was sitting at the end of the table, Constance was leaning in close to him, her hands clasped, a cigarette burning in the ashtray beside her. She had her back to me. Howard was frowning. He was out of his depth. He hated that feeling, and he dealt with it by asking questions. I didn't want her telling him that Morgan murdered someone.

—Howard, I need to speak to Constance alone, I said.

She began to turn her head. She wasn't pleased to be interrupted. In her face, as she peered at me over her shoulder, I saw sheer malevolence and loathing. Again I didn't recognize her. Howard was happy to escape. I closed the kitchen door and sat down at the table.

—It's not fair on him, I said. He's not old enough.

—He's old enough to know what was done to me.

—No, Constance, he's not, not yet. He's still a child. Let him have a few more years of innocence.

Her eyebrows flicked up as she reached for her cigarette. She planted it in the corner of her mouth. She hooded her eyelids against the smoke. For a moment she looked like Barb's mother, old Queenie Mulcahy. But at least Queenie never lost her sense of humor. She kept it alive with gin.

—He's still innocent, you mean.

Unspoken was the thought, Fortunate child. We should all be so lucky.

—That's what I do mean. Tell me something.

—What, Sidney?

—How do you propose to get the house back?

She dropped her eyes. She crushed the cigarette out. I didn't need to tell her she had no money. She didn't even have a job. Then she looked up, straightened her back, and pushed her hands through her hair in a way I knew well. She turned her face up to the ceiling and closed her eyes. It marked a change of mood, a shift to the positive.

—Oh, Sidney, Sidney. So practical always. So very orderly in all you do.

She gazed at me full on, direct and intense.

—I'll find a way, she said.

I nodded.

—But I want to ask you something, she said.

—What is it?

—Take me up there one last time. I think it would help. And Mildred must be so lonely.

What was going on now? I didn't trust her. Mildred had become an object of contempt in Constance's mind and Ravenswood was a kind of mausoleum, its sole relic the spirit of Daddy and his attendant ghost. Her only thought for weeks had been to destroy it. Why did she want to see it one last time, if not to set it ablaze?

But I didn't say this. I no longer had the will to go up against her. She was too strong for me. She was starting to get the better of me.

—Sure.

—When?

—When the car's fixed.

There'd been more trouble with the Jag. Having performed reliably, more than reliably, magnificently, for many years, like everything else it was beginning to fail. Replacement parts had to be sent over from England. It would be in the garage for at least a month.

—We can take the train.

—Let's talk about it later.

But she hated to be thwarted. She had no tolerance for delay.

—Why can't we talk about it now, is there a reason not to talk about it now? You think I'll forget about it if we don't talk about it now? You think I'm a fool?

—Please, Constance.

She was working herself into a rage. Her eyes were glazed, her lips moving rapidly, silently.

—*Please?*

—All right. When do you want to go?

—Saturday morning so Howard can come.

That was the Tuesday. I had less than four days. I went back to my study and picked up the manuscript of *A Scream in the Night: Hysteria and the Moral Collapse of a Great American City*.

★

The heat wave didn't let up. It occurred to me that it might be good for Constance to revisit the house after all. Her fixed idea about her childhood might undergo some modification. Not every memory was a bad one. Life is more complicated, more *nuanced* than the obsessive mind will allow. I began to convince myself that yes, it was a good thing that she return. Ed Kaplan was with me on this.

—You're being smart, he said, all those good times she had with her sister, they must mean something.

—Iris died up there.

—I know that. It doesn't mean there aren't happy memories. And she loved her mother.

Yes, she loved her mother. I allowed myself to become guardedly optimistic. But life remained intensely uncomfortable. It was still hard to sleep in that heat. There was a standing fan in every room in the apartment but there was never enough of a draft. It didn't improve the mood on the street, but I tried to shut out the screaming and the sirens and entertain a vision of homecoming and reconciliation. I saw us arrive upstate on a clear day when the breezes off the mountains had cleansed the air, and the river sparkled in the sunlight as Mildred emerged from the house to greet us, not an old ghost, no, but a woman at peace with the world, and fulfilled, living in the house she'd inherited from the man she'd so loyally served. She'd found the means to make repairs, to bring in men, carpenters and painters, so the place was bright and trim to the eye, and inside all was fresh and spotless. Mildred was nothing if not a housekeeper and this, now, was her house. She would welcome us to it with modest pride.

As I tossed and turned in the damp night heat, in the airless, claustrophobic little bedroom behind the kitchen I imagined all this, and I saw Constance embrace Mildred as Howard ran across the grass, his arms spread wide—

There would be talk then of an extended stay, for Ravenswood was too big for one woman, and it surely needed a child's laughter to bring it fully back to life, and Constance turned to me, radiant, saying I could have the tower for my library, and I knew then that her nightmare was over, that she'd finally come home—

Wednesday. Every window was open. Every fan was turning. Constance sat at the kitchen table in a light bathrobe open over her underwear. Gladys didn't come in on a Wednesday. Howard was at school. Her hair was piled untidily on top of her head. She was fanning herself with a magazine. She was looking at family photographs, the English mama in her garden, various dogs, herself, Iris. Daddy. I saw her go through the heap of photos as though it were a deck of cards. I believe she was looking, not for the first time, for a glimpse of a tall blond youth, her father. A cigarette hung from the corner of her mouth. She was frowning. Her glasses were on the end of her nose. She was wearing a lace-edged brassiere under the flimsy nightgown and it lent a nice clean definition to her small pert breasts. Her hair was damp and drops of perspiration glistened on the back of her neck. I leaned over and kissed her neck where it was sweaty and tasted salt.

—What are you doing?

She was slapping the photos down like a widow playing solitaire. My hands were on her shoulders now. I was starting to pant a little. I slid my hands down to her breasts.

—Stop it, she said.

But her attention was on the photographs.

I pressed my lips to her neck again. I pushed the nightdress off her shoulders. She twisted her head around to look at me. I tried to kiss her mouth but she averted her face from me.

—Stand up, I whispered.

She sighed, then stood up and faced me. The nightgown had fallen to her elbows but it couldn't fall further because her arms were folded.

—Why are you making that noise? she said.

I gently pushed her arms apart and pressed myself to her body. Surprisingly passive now, she leaned back against the table, her hands splayed on the surface behind her. A few photographs drifted to the floor. I unloosed my trousers. They fell to my ankles. My hands were pressed to the cool damp flesh of her back and my face was buried in her neck. Her hair was starting to come loose. Up came the greedy trout. I was breathing fast and shallow now and whispering her name over and over, then with a shock like lightning or electricity my fingers brushed the warm lips of her vulva—

—I don't know if I want to do this, she said loudly.

—You do, I whispered.

It made her laugh.

—You want to do it here?

I did. I wanted to do it here, now, right in the here and now.

—All right, Sidney.

She pulled her underpants aside and arranged herself canted slightly backwards against the edge of the table, with her hands on my shoulders, murmuring distractedly about the heat in the apartment, hissing at me to slow down.

—Now you can, she said.

After a few seconds she told me to call her Iris and I was encouraged. But she was disengaged throughout: I stared at her face while it was happening. She gazed at the ceiling with a blank expression and it was over too quickly. Only once did she produce a small gasp, and that's what did it for me, that mere brief involuntary intake of breath, which was followed by a word, or a name, I didn't hear it clearly, was it *Daddy*? It wasn't *Sidney*, or *darling*, or *love*—

—What a mess you've made, she remarked. And a little after that she said: Well, that was incandescent.

I was beyond caring by then. It was sex, but it was like sex with a mannequin, apart from the gasp. *Incandescent.* I thought she might have destroyed the last of my love with that one word, I didn't even care about the *Daddy.* Perhaps it was *Eddie?* That would be something. But I wouldn't know the damage she'd done until later. These things either burn slowly through tissue like acid or you shake them off with a careless laugh. She left the kitchen. I stood leaning over the sink, gripping the sides and panting, as I ran the water cold. I was suddenly very thirsty.

That was Wednesday.

Thursday was uneventful. She was cool with me. Neither of us made reference to the incident at the kitchen table. That evening it occurred to me after Howard had gone to bed that if we tried again we might do better. I suggested it.

—Not tonight, darling, she said.

I think she was laughing at me. What I heard was: Not any night, darling. Not any day. Not at the kitchen table, not in bed, nowhere. Never. Her scorn and her insults hadn't killed my love, however: the reverse. I wanted her very much, more than ever if that was possible. I remembered how I felt the night I met her, when we'd sat in an empty restaurant and she told me about her family. I'd listened to her story, all the while ravenous, hungering for her, thinking it incredible that I might have this pale distant vision of a girl with her porcelain limbs and startled eyes and her sudden throaty laughter—

This is what we'd come to. Incandescent. And then for the first time, I don't know why, perhaps remembering the night I met her and the promise I felt then, the anticipation, it occurred to me that I might share some responsibility for what had happened to us, was this possible? I mean that some part at least of our trouble was my doing? Briefly I glimpsed a seed or germ of an idea here, perhaps not the truth, or not the whole truth, but *something*. I remembered what Barb used to say about my *control tendencies*, my *dogmatic inflexibility*—

More than once Ed Kaplan had told me I couldn't take criticism. But that way madness lay. No, I was in the right here. Surely.

Friday was eventful. I asked where the family photos were, the ones she'd spread all over the kitchen table, and she said she'd thrown them in the trash. I asked her what happened to the trash and she said it had already gone down. The destruction of photographs is an act of spiritual violence. Mildred Knapp burned the photographs of her husband, Walter, and deprived Constance of knowing what the man she believed to be her father looked like. Now she'd done the same. They were all dead, of course, but it was tantamount to a second death, an end to their lives in her memory. I tried to tell her this.

—It's none of your business, she said.

—Did you throw out our wedding photos?

—Yes.

—Then it is my business.

We were in the bedroom for this conversation. I'd gone in to find a clean shirt. She tried to leave but I blocked the door.

—You'd like to throw me out, I said. You'd like me to fall under a train.

—Let me go, please.

—Why are we doing this, Constance?

—What?

—Keeping up this sham of a marriage.

—I thought you wanted it.

I stepped away from the door and sat on the bed. She left the room. Why did she act like this? Then: Why did I act like this? Why didn't I just take her in my arms like the petulant child she was and give her what she needed, I mean tender love and affection and sympathy and understanding? That was in the morning, around ten.

We had an argument in the afternoon, a bad one. I told her she was a hysteric. She called me passive-aggressive. Neither of us emerged well from this ugly skirmish. I started it. I'd grown impatient with forbearance. Her hostility was fierce and unwavering and I'd done nothing to deserve it. I didn't care anymore what had soured that woman's soul. I'd tried to be a good determinist and see her as the victim of a vindictive stepfather but my heart was never really in it because at root I believe each one of us makes our own destiny by choosing whether or not to *remain* the victim of our childhood. Hers didn't seem to me to be so very terrible, and I said this in the course of our horrid argument and of course it was destructive because Constance saw herself as a woman brutally deprived of a father's love, a perception she'd allowed to color all her dealings with the world. She was a bitter, unpleasant person, I told her, and she made others unhappy, and she'd been a great disappointment to me and not even Howard's welfare was enough to keep me in this marriage any longer.

There was a sudden silence. Was I going to leave her? I'd never said that to her before, even after she betrayed me. But I was saying it now. The silence lasted for a few astonished seconds and I waited to see if she'd break down and melt my anger with her tears. She didn't. Instead my words were like oil spilled on the flames that burned in her angry heart and she screamed at me for a while before I realized that Howard would be home from school at any moment and that I'd better get away from her so the boy didn't see us like this. I was leaving the building just as he came along the block. He saw that I was upset. He asked me if we were still going to Ravenswood in the morning. I knew he was looking forward to it. It was a family outing and he didn't get too many of those. Of course we are, I told him.

I walked for an hour in Central Park. Eventually I found a place on the grass and lay down amid the sunbathers and the guitar players and the lovers, young and old, and all the other New Yorkers who wanted to be anywhere but inside. Central Park, the lungs of the city. It was still hot in the late afternoon, but not as hot as it would be in an apartment, all the more so if you were implicated in the terminal convulsions of a failing marriage. Central

Park was preferable to that all right. I lay on my back and watched the sky and asked myself what I was going to do, and how much time I had, and was I really so sure I was in the right. My certainties had been shaken after the *incandescent* debacle and I sensed that in the darkness large structures were beginning to collapse.

We spent the evening as usual. After an almost silent dinner in the kitchen we went to the sitting room where Howard was eager to beat Constance at chess. To my surprise she'd won three games in a row. I wouldn't have picked her for a chess player, but of course to a devious, paranoid woman like Constance chess would come easy. Chess is made for people like Constance. There it was again, and for the third time I experienced doubt. I attempted to quell it. Didn't I know my own mind? I was reading through the few finished pages of *A Scream in the Night* and it occurred to me that I might blame New York City for the collapse of my marriage, or the polluted waters of the Hudson River, any damn thing if I shared Constance's philosophy, but no, it was trite and shallow thinking. I knew what had gone wrong, and strangely enough it was a problem she'd indentified early in the marriage: It was her *repetition compulsion complex.* She'd married her father. Then she'd realized what she'd done and wanted out. I should have let her go as soon as she said it, but I didn't take her seriously. She'd never been able to see me as other than patriarchal, a controlling, withholding father figure. I didn't believe I was guilty of any of this but she did, and she made trouble so that I *became* controlling and withholding and in this way validated her conviction that I was just like Daddy, or that I *was* Daddy, at least in her unconscious mind. And

Constance's unconscious mind was a dank and dripping cellar that harbored various punitive archetypes, the result being that she never even attempted to see how I differed from Morgan Schuyler in reality. At the same time she refused to visit a psychiatrist. She didn't want to change. She was terrified of change. She'd once said to me: You change or you die. But her existence was grounded in her hatred of Daddy and she didn't know how to live without it. She was afraid to be free.

As I'd lain on the grass in the park earlier, listening to the plinky-plonky banjos and the reedy tuneless voices, I'd realized that Constance would never sing freedom's song. She'd surrendered her autonomy. She showed no defiance, no resistance, she was constrained in bands of steel of her own making. She was trapped. She'd been silent when I told her that not even Howard could keep me in this marriage. That silence was her admission that she needed me. But she only needed me in order to hate me. That's what she did to fathers, she hated them. Not her fantasy father, of course, not Walter Knapp, the blond whispering ghost who feared nothing and died for the honor of the English mama, oh no, she didn't hate him, she romanticized him, she idealized him, him she could love because she didn't have to deal with him in the real world. But I'd had enough. It was disheartening to think that I'd lost a third marriage but it was too bad. It was impossible to go on this way.

Saturday morning we were up at dawn to catch the early train upstate. I still didn't trust Constance's motives for this visit to Ravenswood but I didn't care anymore. I was doing it for Howard. I didn't know how I'd break it to him that the marriage was over. I'd spent half the night in my stifling airless cell trying to figure it out. But living with Constance for Howard's sake was no longer feasible. About this at least I was resolved.

She made him breakfast and I saw that her mood had changed in the night. The brooding shrew was gone, in her place the bright, brittle hausfrau with a plan in her mind and a timetable to keep to. After breakfast she asked me to please go to the corner and get us a cab to take us to Penn Station. She and Howard would be waiting in the lobby. It was another very hot day. I was wearing light trousers, striped blue suspenders, a white shirt, a gay bow tie, tennis shoes, and a Panama hat. It was a good Panama. I'd bought it in a store across the street from Macy's and it wasn't cheap. Constance was wearing a white summer frock and flat shoes. She had a straw hat with a gaily colored ribbon, and sunglasses. Howard was wearing shorts and sandals and a white cotton shirt. He had sunglasses and a floppy beach hat and she'd smeared cream on his face because his delicate milky skin burned in the sun. She was very attentive to him now. A few nights earlier, after he'd gone to bed, she said she didn't want him catching her disease. I said, what disease, and she said, Daddy's disease. I didn't pursue it.

I went down in the elevator to get us a cab. There were no cabs. It was inexplicable. There were always cabs. It was Saturday morning, that must be the reason. I looked at my watch. I had to make a decision. I walked back along the block and found Constance and Howard waiting in the lobby. I told them we'd have to take the subway to Penn Station. Constance was furious with me but she didn't make a scene in front of Howard. But she knew it would be humid down there and we'd be dripping with sweat before we even got to Penn Station.

237

We went into the subway and narrowly missed a downtown train. Constance was no longer so brisk and brittle. My failure to find a cab had upset her plans. Now we were all perspiring. She was mopping Howard's face with a handkerchief and although she was wearing sunglasses, and I couldn't see her eyes, I felt her rage. The train didn't come. The minutes ticked by. People kept arriving on the platform, more and more of them, and it got very close down there, and too densely crowded for us to get back up to the street easily. We were packed in together like sardines in a can as far back as the turnstiles, and the temperature continued inexorably to rise.

I checked my watch again. I was worried about finding the ticket office in Penn Station. Then I heard a downtown train approaching in the tunnel. The crowd moved forward. Constance was pressed against my back. She clutched my shirt with both hands. She was terrified, she felt she'd be crushed, she became claustrophobic in any public space with a crowd of people around her, I'd seen it happen. She gripped me tight as the crowd shifted and again forced us forward toward the oncoming train. My Panama came off and reaching for it I stumbled.

TWELVE

SIDNEY'S HAT FELL off and I saw him stumble as he reached for it. He was very close to the edge of the platform. I turned away and covered my face with my hands but I didn't scream. I was with Howard. I didn't want to alarm him. The crowd was moving forward, trying to get to the train like a great ponderous unthinking animal or a slow, heaving tide, irresistible and mindless. Then I saw Howard going under, I saw his arm lifted and I heard a cry of panic, so I did what any mother would do and I lunged forward and swept him up in my arms and clutched him tight to my body. I was being pushed and jostled from all sides now but I didn't move. I refused to move. I stood resolute with my back to the train and my child in my arms, a rock in the stream. They didn't like it, they were desperate to reach the train, there was no knowing when there'd be another one.

Then I began to push against the moving crowd. I had to, to get him out of there. The child was terrified. I lifted him so he was high above their heads and able at least to breathe. I shouted to him, asking him if he was okay, and a man in a thin tie with his collar unbuttoned and sweat-stained collided with me and for a second his furious face was close to mine and in his wild eyes I saw depths of rage and misery even as he muttered at me to get out of his goddamn way. Howard shouted that yes he was okay, and Papa was right behind us. He was right behind us, he hadn't fallen onto the tracks, and it was a relief to hear that at least. I heard the train pulling out of the station and the great herd, what remained of it, subsided and grew quiet and we were at last able to move. Sidney joined us as we found the exit. Then together we climbed the steps to the street.

The air was oppressively humid and the sky was black. A cab pulled up and a man came leaping out of it and ran into the subway. We clambered into the cab and Sidney told the driver to take us to Penn Station. We fell back against the seat and Sidney heaved a sigh and reached for my hand, thanking me. I guess it was because I'd taken care of Howard but what did he expect? We were quiet as the cab rushed down Broadway. I was glad that Sidney was safe. I told him so. I meant it. Below Columbus Circle the driver took Seventh Avenue and so we continued downtown through that strange thundery day.

Penn Station was far along in its destruction. Above the grimy facade rose a frame of steel girders and a towering crane. Scaffolding clung to the exterior wall in the few places where the granite hadn't yet been torn away. We climbed a wooden staircase. Travelers sat in the waiting room beneath billowing tarpaulins. They browsed in stores that sold souvenirs and candies and magazines. It was a travesty of normality in that huge ruin with its deafening crashes of steel on steel and its shouting men. Sidney went off to buy our tickets. Standing with Howard in the cacophony I became disturbed and had to press my hands to my ears. He hated it too.

—Howard, I shouted, let's get out of here.

We went back down the wooden staircase and retraced our steps through the taxi entrance to the street. The storm was about to break. I knew by then that I wouldn't go back to Ravenswood. I'd never go back.

—Let's take a walk, I said.

—What about Papa?

—Papa will find us.

Hand in hand we walked away from the station. A few minutes later we stood in front of the Dunmore Hotel. It was closed now. I felt the sadness that decrepitude arouses when you see an empty structure no longer useful or attractive to anyone. That would be me one day, I thought. One day soon. And was I then to be alone? I felt a first few drops of rain on my skin.

—Come on, kiddo, I said, let's see what it looks like inside.

Was I to be alone?

We were standing under the canopy at the top of the steps when the rain came sweeping down with sudden violence. As we gazed out into the deluge, lightning flickered in the black clouds and then came a peal of thunder very close overhead and very loud. The street was brilliantly illuminated for a second or two and in that strange light I saw the tenements and fire escapes and the line of long, low, beat-up automobiles parked along the curb opposite. A few bent, scurrying figures clutching newspapers over their heads fled along the sidewalk. They were seeking shelter in doorways and stores.

I banged at the door of the hotel. It was opened. The old man recognized me and let us in.

—It's Miss Constance, he said.

—Hello, Simon.

The doorman. He told me they'd kept him on as a caretaker until the demolition began. I said I wanted to take a look at the place one last time. He told me how sorry he was to hear about my sister. He was genuinely distressed. I thanked him. The lobby was empty and all the furniture had gone. The rain continued heavy. I took Howard through to the cocktail lounge. A few chairs stood against the wall and the piano was still there but little else. I sat in my usual booth and Howard wandered away. The room seemed much larger than it had before. I lit a cigarette.

I thought about Iris. How could I not? I saw her as she was before the affair with Eddie ended, Iris in that absurd red cocktail dress, flaunting her body to the world. Sidney believed I'd caused her death. Perhaps I had. I didn't realize her heart was so fragile. Howard played a note on the piano. I looked up and he was standing with his mouth open, staring at the ceiling. The note he'd played hung in the dusty gloom then slowly died away. I thought about Eddie Castrol, who had no heart at all. Impurity is contagious and so are secrets. It's not the dead who haunt us, it's the empty space they leave inside us with their secrets: the crypt. Then Sidney appeared in the doorway. I'd almost lost him.

He'd known where to find us. Howard saw him before I did. He ran across the empty room, then he was clinging to his father's legs. Sidney put his hand on the boy's head. He was looking at me where I sat smoking in the booth with the red plush upholstery. Detaching Howard from his legs he came over and sat down beside me. His clothes were wet and so was his hair, and with his shirt and trousers glued to his body he looked like a wild mad hobo and he moved me. Now he was gazing at me like he used to in the early days before the wedding when he was still in love with me. I hadn't seen that face in such a long time. It had gone badly wrong with us but I didn't want it to fall apart now, no I did not, I was exhausted and so was he. He'd suffered enough. He'd paid for what was done to me and I couldn't ask him to do more. He put his hand in his pocket and laid three damp railroad tickets on the table. I shook my head.

—No? he said.

—Never again.

He took my fingers to his lips and held them there with his eyes closed. What a sentimental man he was. Howard watched us for a few seconds then returned to the piano. I heard a chord this time then it too died in the ceiling. The boy stood at the keyboard looking at us. He played the chord again.

—What do you want to do now? said Sidney.

—Go home with you.

—And Howard?

I didn't want to say the words aloud. Instead I mouthed them: *I'm his mother now.*

He seemed not to understand. I did it again.

243

A NOTE ON THE AUTHOR

Patrick McGrath is the author of a short story
collection, *Blood and Water and Other Tales,* and seven
previous novels including *Asylum, Martha Peake, Port
Mungo* and *Trauma,* shortlisted for the Costa Novel
Award. He has also published *Ghost Town,* a volume
of novellas about New York. *Spider* was made into a
film in 2002 by acclaimed director David Cronenberg.
Patrick McGrath lives in London and New York.

A NOTE ON THE TYPE

The text of this book is set in Bembo. This type was first used in 1495 by the Venetian printer Aldus Manutius for Cardinal Bembo's *De Aetna*, and was cut for Manutius by Francesco Griffo. It was one of the types used by Claude Garamond (1480–1561) as a model for his Romain de L'Université, and so it was the forerunner of what became standard European type for the following two centuries. Its modern form follows the original types and was designed for Monotype in 1929.